"Now, how do you suppose my dress got into your closet?" Mom asked.

"Maybe you put it there by mistake—"

"Never mind. I know it's just another of your tricks to keep me from dating Grant." Mom shook her head, and her beautiful brownish-red hair rippled over her shoulders. "Don't you know you can't keep us apart?"

Ginger shrugged, feeling sorry for herself. Wasn't it bad enough to be what people called "a product of divorce"? Wasn't it bad enough that her mother was beautiful? That her hair was brownish-red like autumn leaves instead of bright red like her own? Did her mother have to go out on dates, too? And did she have to fall in love with Grant Gabriel, when she could probably marry Dad again?

Here Comes GINGER!

The Ginger Series
by Elaine L. Schulte

Here Comes Ginger!
Off to a New Start
A Job for an Angel
Absolutely Green
Go For It!

Here Comes GINGER!

Elaine L. Schulte

Chariot Books™
David C. Cook Publishing Co.

A White Horse Book
Published by Chariot Books,™
an imprint of David C. Cook Publishing Co.
David C. Cook Publishing Co., Elgin, Illinois
David C. Cook Publishing Co., Weston, Ontario

HERE COMES GINGER!
© 1989 by Elaine L. Schulte

Cover design by Ad/Plus, Ltd.
Cover illustration by Janice Skivington
First printing, 1989
Printed in the United States of America
98 97 96 95 94   10 9 8 7 6 5 4

Library of Congress Cataloging-in-Publication Data

Schulte, Elaine L.
  Here comes Ginger! / Elaine L. Schulte.
    p.   cm.—(A White horse book) (A Ginger book)
  Summary: Ten-year-old Ginger reacts badly to her mother's plans
to remarry, but after a great deal of anguish, God grants her peace
and acceptance.
  ISBN 1-55513-770-9
  [1. Remarriage—Fiction. 2. Christian life—Fiction.]   I. Title.
II. Series: Schulte, Elaine L. Ginger book.
PZ7.S3867He   1989
[Fic]—dc19   88-38763
                                                        CIP
                                                        AC

To Laura,
with a heart full of love

1

Ginger shoved a stick of gum into her mouth and stuck the crushed foil in the pocket of her brown shorts. Chewing faster and faster, she started down the hall to her bedroom.

"Ginger Anne Trumbell!" her mother called out. "Where did you hide my new dress?"

Ginger raced down the hallway and ducked into what her mother called "a brown cave of a bedroom." She nearly knocked over the flimsy wooden chair as she sat down at her desk. Grabbing a book, she opened it and stared at the blur of words.

In trouble again, she thought, and gave her gum a loud crack.

"Ginger?" Mom repeated.

She pretended not to hear. She hated the sound of her name. It reminded her of her freckles, wild red curls, and cat green eyes. Worst of all, it reminded her of her temper.

"Ginger!"

She turned toward the doorway and widened her eyes.

"There you are," Mom said. She stepped into the room, still wearing her blue-and-white striped robe.

"Yes, Mom?"

"Please, Ginger, don't use that innocent look on me."

She had expected her mother to be angrier, but her blue eyes softened and her dimples deepened. She was trying to be patient, that's what it was. Maybe she wouldn't even mention what a mess the room was, or how disgusting it was to hear gum crack. Everything was different with Mom lately. You never knew what to expect from her.

"Where did you hide my new dress?" her mother asked again.

Ginger tried to sound innocent. "Which dress?"

"You know very well which dress. The white lacy one I bought for my date tonight."

"Maybe you left it at the cleaners, or—"

"Or maybe it's in your closet?" Mom interrupted. She headed for the closet and opened the door.

Hangers scraped and clattered, and Ginger braced herself against the chair, prepared to be caught.

"And here it is!" Mom announced, sounding like

Papa Bear finding Goldilocks. She turned with a mischievous smile. "Ginger snaps again!"

Uff! She hated gingersnap jokes.

"Now, how do you suppose my dress got into your closet?" Mom asked.

"Maybe you put it there by mistake—"

"Never mind. I know it's just another of your tricks to keep me from dating Grant Gabriel." She shook her head, and her beautiful brownish-red hair rippled over her shoulders. "Don't you know you can't keep Grant and me apart?"

Ginger shrugged, feeling sorry for herself. Wasn't it bad enough to be what people called "a product of divorce"? Wasn't it bad enough that her mother was beautiful? That her hair was brownish-red like autumn leaves instead of bright red like her own? Did her mother have to go out on dates, too? And did she have to start falling in love with Grant Gabriel when she could probably marry Dad again?

Mom stood in front of her. "Don't you have anything to say for yourself?"

"I'm sorry, Mom."

"I know life hasn't been easy for you these past few years," her mother said. Her dimples deepened again, and she patted Ginger's shoulder. "You're forgiven."

"I am?" Ginger asked.

"Yup, you are. I understand."

Ginger stared at her freckled kneecaps and almost wished Mom would yell the way she used to.

11

"I'm making pizza for your dinner," Mom said, "cheese and pepperoni, your favorite." With that, she whisked happily out of the room, her white dress held high and so carefully it might have been a wedding gown. "By the way," she added from the hallway, "you're reading that book upside down."

Ginger let out a muffled "Uff!" and slammed the book shut. Seeing it was *Incredible Journey*, she felt even worse. Her best friend, Mandy Timmons, had given it to her last week before moving from Santa Rosita to Chicago. Everyone thought Mandy's family was crazy, moving away from southern California—and at the beginning of summer vacation! And as if that weren't enough, Mom had to be falling in love.

Ginger's thoughts returned to the dress. A good thing she hadn't been caught trying it on. Not that it made her look grown-up or anything. It had drooped like a sack on her straight up-and-down body. Just one of the problems of being almost eleven years old.

She leaned back in her desk chair, then tipped forward, then back, and forward again. Hiding the dress hadn't been too smart, but she'd dream up something better. She'd never let Mom fall entirely in love with Grant Gabriel. Not if she could help it.

For a long time Ginger sat teetering back and forth and cracking her gum. Maybe a plan would come if she made a list. She opened her top desk drawer and scrounged through the mess. Finding a lined tablet, she plopped it on her scarred maple desk and wrote, *How to stop Mom's date tonight.*

As she tapped her pencil on the desk, an idea struck. She'd let out the air from Grant's tires!

The air fizzed from the idea with a fast *pffft*, and she felt like a flat tire herself. Dumb, dumb, dumb, dumb. They'd know right away she'd done it. And if she ruined Grant's tires, she'd really be in trouble.

If only Mandy hadn't moved. She always came up with good ideas. She'd write to her. Anyhow, she should thank her for *Incredible Journey*, even if she hadn't read it yet.

Ginger cracked her gum loudly again. Maybe she'd say she felt sick. That might keep Mom home. She really did feel sick whenever Mom and Grant looked at each other lately. *Lovesick* was what they were. Playing sick herself wouldn't be too far from the truth . . . or was it?

"A lie is a lie," Mom said now. She used to tell little white lies herself, but not anymore. Grant Gabriel was so good, he'd been a terrible influence on her. He'd even gotten Mom to become a Christian, and she hadn't been the same since.

Ginger plopped her chair down on all four legs and looked around her room. It was really a mess, piled with clothes, stuffed animals, her seashell collection, and other junk, but it felt right to her. At least with Mom's life changing, she didn't always harp about cleaning the room anymore.

"Pizza's ready!" Mom called from the kitchen.

13

The smell of melting cheese and hot pepperoni wafted into her bedroom and brought Ginger to her feet. If there was one food in the world she loved, it was p-i-z-z-a.

"Coming!"

In the kitchen, Mom still wore her robe. "Pizza for dinner and fudge nut brownies for dessert. What do you think of that?"

Sure enough, a plate with three big brownies waited on the counter. Their chocolaty smell mingled with the mouth-watering aroma of pizza.

"Mmmmm," Ginger said, settling herself on a kitchen stool. "Thanks a lot!"

"I've wrapped more brownies for you to take to Gram's."

"She'll like that," Ginger answered and watched for her mother to turn her back. The instant she turned, Ginger stuck her wad of gum under the counter, then helped herself to a slice of pizza. It burned her fingers a little, but she felt so hungry it didn't even matter if she burned the roof of her mouth.

When her mother finished rinsing dishes, she stood and watched.

"Aren't you going to eat, Mom?"

"Grant is taking me out for dinner." She hesitated, then said, "You know, Ginger, he has a big house."

Ginger's mouth was full of cheese and pepperoni, but she asked, "A big house?"

14

"Yes, a very big house . . . and the guest bedroom is such a cheerful yellow. It'd be just right for you."

Ginger nearly choked. "I don't want another bedroom! I like mine just fine!"

"His guest room would look so beautiful with a white canopied bed," her mother added. "You'd be like a princess in it. I could stencil flowers around the ceiling—"

"I don't want a yellow bedroom! I like brown just fine. And I don't want flowers or anything stenciled anywhere!"

Her mother gave her a strange smile, then closed her eyes and turned away.

Probably praying as usual, Ginger decided.

She bit into her pizza again and didn't enjoy it quite as much. She liked her brown cave of a room with its brown plaid wallpaper and brown carpet and brown bedspread. Brown was bright enough for a redhead who was all knees and legs and elbows. As for playing princess, the idea was double dumb.

"Well, I'd better get dressed," her mother said.

Ginger watched her leave the kitchen. *You'd think she'd want to stay in this house*, Ginger thought. Sure it was little and old-fashioned, but it'd been just fine before Mom met Grant Gabriel.

Ginger eyed the white kitchen. Mom had stenciled red hearts on the cabinets and a matching ceiling border. Her friends said, "How charming you've made it, Sallie. You've turned the kitchen into a

15

gem." After that, Mom went crazy with decorating. She'd painted her bedroom and stenciled a daisy ceiling border, and then came trailing green ivy in the hallway. Now Grant wanted her to stencil in his house. He'd said, "With your flair for decorating, you ought to take classes. Who knows, you might be a budding artist."

The more Ginger considered her problems, the worse the pizza tasted. She didn't even try the brownies. Instead, she collected her gum from under the counter and popped it back into her mouth. Chewing fast, she headed for her room. If only Mom hadn't worked as a temporary secretary for Grant Gabriel at Santa Rosita Christian School.

At her desk, Ginger grabbed her pencil and crossed out *How to stop Mom's date tonight*. Below it, she wrote, *How to stop Mom and Grant from falling worse in love*.

She had no more than written it than . . . vroom . . . an idea hit.

She'd stop being polite to him. That's it! She'd be so awful that Grant Gabriel would never visit Mom again. After all, who'd want to date a woman with a bratty kid? Giving her gum a determined crack, she knew that she'd found the answer. Ginger Anne Trumbell would snap again!

2

"Grant's here! Time to leave!" Mom called out.

"Just a minute!" In her bedroom, Ginger brushed the green Magic Marker felt tip over her last fingernail. Now all ten of her nails glowed. Recapping the tube, she yelled, "Coming!" She grabbed her book and her stuffed green parrot, and headed down the hallway.

Now, to get on Grant's nerves, she told herself. Maybe it wouldn't be easy with a principal. He probably put up with a lot, even in a Christian high school.

Grant Gabriel rose from the couch as Ginger entered the room. He wore a grayish-blue summer suit, the shade of his eyes. His wavy brown hair and nice smile made him look handsome, even if he was older than Dad. As for Mom, she looked perfect in her white lacy dress and white high-heeled sandals.

"Hello, Ginger," Grant said with a nod. "How are you this evening?"

He sounded interested, but that wasn't going to stop her. "Terrible," she snapped.

"Ginger—" her mother warned, then her glance dropped to Ginger's hands. "What have you done to your fingernails?"

Ginger gazed at them, unconcerned. "Oh . . . I thought for a second I'd smeared it."

"Why, Ginger," Grant said, "how good you look with green fingernails! They match your lovely eyes."

Match my lovely eyes?!

"Which reminds me," he continued, pleasant as ever, "I've brought you a present. Something I know you can use."

Probably more stationery, she thought as she accepted the gift-wrapped box. She already had three boxes of it, mostly unused. "Thanks," she managed.

"Go ahead, open it," he said.

She ripped off the wrapping paper. "Chewing gum! You're giving me chewing gum???"

"I know you enjoy it," he said. "No sense in giving people things they don't enjoy. Isn't that right, Sallie?"

"I suppose so," Mom answered and smiled at him.

"Guess we'd better be on our way," he said.

"We'll drop you off at your grandmother's house, Ginger."

"I always walk," Ginger objected. "You know that. Gram only lives a block away."

"It'll put your mother's mind at ease if we drive you," Grant replied firmly. "Don't forget your gum."

Ginger stuffed two packs of gum into her shorts pocket, tucked Parrot back under her arm, and grabbed her book.

Mom carried the plastic-wrapped plate of brownies, and Grant held the front door open for them. He bowed as if it were a special occasion. "Ladies?"

Mom replied, beaming, "Thank you, kind sir."

Yuck, Ginger thought. *Yuck and double yuck.*

Grant's pale blue four-door Oldsmobile waited at the curb behind Mom's shabby brown two-door Ford. Ginger climbed into the backseat, wondering why she'd turned dumb instead of nasty. Was it Grant giving her the gum? Or his mentioning her "lovely green eyes"? Well, she wouldn't give up. And now she had a far better idea. She'd ask Dad to help.

"Comfortable, Sallie?" Grant asked as they settled into the car.

"Perfectly, thanks," Mom answered happily.

Ginger turned away and stuck a fresh stick of gum in her mouth. Chewing hard, she stared at their old two-bedroom house on its narrow city lot.

19

It wasn't much, but she sure didn't want Mom to get married and move them away from the beach.

As they drove off, Ginger waited for a chance to make her announcement. Finally they were quiet, and she said, "Dad will be at Gram's house."

"Really?" her mother replied. "I'm glad to hear he'll be spending time with you, Ginger."

"He's fortunate to have such a fine daughter," Grant said. "Fathers are especially fond of daughters. I know I'm certainly fond of Lilabet . . . and of Joshua, too, of course."

Oh, no! Now he'll start in about his kids! Ginger was glad to see they were already pulling up at Gram's house. There was Dad's red sports car in the driveway. "See, he's here now."

"Would you like us to take you inside?" Grant asked.

"No thanks!" Ginger said. She climbed out so fast Grant couldn't help her, even if she did have to juggle Parrot and her book as she took the brownies.

"Be sure to be home tomorrow morning by eight-thirty," Mom said. "We're going to Grant's father's church and then to a barbecue at the house."

"Since when?" Ginger asked.

Her mother threw her a happy kiss. "Since now."

Grant had gotten out of the car in time to close Ginger's door. "Have a good time," he said.

"Thanks a lot," she tried to snap at him.

"My pleasure," he returned.

After shooting a nasty look at him, she hurried up

20

the sidewalk to Gram's house. When she finally turned, they had pulled away from the curb. Mom wasn't even looking back.

Ginger stepped up onto the porch as Gram opened the door. Her brown eyes danced to see her, and she looked as perky as her halo of salt-and-pepper curls. "There you are, Ginger. Come in. I'm making pizza for supper."

"None for me, thanks," Ginger said, though it did smell good.

"You're saying no to pizza?" Gram asked.

"Well, maybe I can eat a little. I just had some at home." She handed over the brownies. "Mom made them for us."

"Please thank her," Gram said. "I notice they dropped you off. Was your mother wearing her new white dress?"

Ginger nodded.

"How did she look?"

"Too beautiful." Seeing that Gram understood, Ginger heaved a sigh. "Where's Dad?"

"Out back, mowing the lawn." Gram shut the front door behind them. "I'm afraid he's not in a good mood. He didn't want to help with the yard again."

Ginger cracked her gum, discouraged. "Oops, sorry, Gram. I forgot your nerves."

"Thanks," Gram said. "You're a good kid."

"Not so good," Ginger objected. As it was, Gram was the good one. She even took care of her without charging a cent. She always told Mom she wanted to do it because she'd be "lost without Ginger" and because it was her son who never paid his child support.

"Go on out back and see if your dad's done," Gram said.

Ginger plopped her book and Parrot on the living room couch, next to piles of fabric for Gram's seamstress work. She'd get Dad interested in Mom again, Ginger vowed to herself.

When she stepped outside, Dad had just finished mowing. She let the screen door slam behind her.

He turned, and his white smile broke like sunshine under his thick dark moustache. "There you are, kiddo!"

"Hi, Dad."

"Steve," he said, "Steve. You know 'Dad' makes me sound old." He ran a hand through his damp curly hair. "I might look hot from mowing the lawn, but I'm still not old."

"Steve," she corrected herself.

"I've been waiting all day to see you," he said.

"Yeah, I'll bet," she answered. He was a salesman, selling surfboards up and down the coast, and had what he called a gift of gab. "I'll bet you've only been here a little while."

Grinning, he grabbed her hair, then bore down on her scalp with a hard knuckle rub. "Who ratted on me—Gram?"

"Nobody!" Ginger yelped as she pulled away

22

from him. "I knew you'd go surfing this morning. It's Saturday."

"Good guess, kiddo . . . another first!" He chuckled and looked her over. "Hey, far out . . . green fingernails!"

"Yeah."

"How about a few games of ping-pong?" he asked. "Or can't you take my beating you today?"

"Beating me? You're on! We'll see who gets beaten!" She headed for the ping-pong table on the small brick patio.

Her dad grabbed the paddles and a ball from the nearby bench. "Now that school's out, I'll bet you've been practicing on that backboard all week."

She laughed. "Maybe I have and maybe I haven't." The truth was she'd been practicing for an hour or two every day.

He bounced the ball across the old green table to her, his eyes sparkling. "Rally for serve!"

She whammed the ball back. It pinged on one side and ponged on the other, back and forth, back and forth. Moving rapidly about, she returned deep shots, inside shots, fast and slow shots. Finally she slammed the ball to his left edge, a whizzer too fast to return.

"Wow, kiddo!" he exclaimed. "You win first serve."

She served the ball fast, and he missed it. The next serve, she put super spin on the ball. His paddle fanned air.

"No fair . . . all that practicing!" He ran a hand through his dark curls again. "Okay, I'm after blood now!"

He slammed the ball to her side—a white blur. One thing about Dad, he was a bad loser. Exactly what would help most when she told him about Mom and Grant.

After they'd finished, he said, "At least I won two out of three from the next world champion."

Ginger grinned. "Looks like I've got to practice more." She could have played harder, but it was better not to make him mad. He had a bad temper, just like her.

They sat down on their favorite brick step.

"So what else is new?" he asked.

Here's my chance, Ginger thought. She grabbed a deep breath. "Mom is getting kind of serious with Grant Gabriel."

"Oh, yeah? Well . . . good for her. I saw them take off. Doesn't drive such a sporty car, does he?"

"I-I guess not." She couldn't believe he didn't care. He'd always acted jealous around Mom, even though she'd given him no reason to be jealous before this.

"I hear Gabriel is stuck with a family to drive around since his wife died in that accident," Dad said. "No wife and two kids to take care of."

"How do you know that?" Ginger asked.

"Word gets around."

"Well . . . don't you even care about Mom?"

"We've been divorced for three years now, kiddo. What she does is her own business, just like what I do is mine."

"I hoped you . . ." She pressed her lips together to keep them from trembling and stared down at her freckled legs.

"You hoped what?" he asked.

Ginger shook her head wordlessly. She hoped he would marry her mother again, that's all. Why . . . oh, why, did they have to get divorced? She'd never understand it. Worst of all, she always felt it was somehow her fault.

"Hang tough, kiddo." He rubbed his hard knuckles over her head again making her yell. "Come on, let's eat some pizza."

Inside, Gram cut the pizza at the dining room table. For the first time ever, the smell of pizza made Ginger feel sick.

Her father turned on the TV. "Let's catch the baseball scores while we eat."

Gram shot her a sympathetic look as they settled at the table. Suddenly her eyes widened. "My land, Ginger, what made you paint your fingernails green?"

"Just wanted to, I guess," Ginger answered.

Gram passed the salad to her. "You must have."

Nobody talked much during dinner, and Ginger only ate one slice of pizza.

"What do you want to do tonight?" Gram looked at Ginger and then at Dad.

"Do?" Ginger's father repeated. "I hope you're not counting on me staying here. I've got a big date."

Gram said, "But I thought you and Ginger could—"

"You thought wrong, Mom."

Gram drew a deep breath. "I see."

Still watching the sports news, they ate the brownies.

When they finished, he stood up from the table. "Can't keep my date waiting. You two have a great week."

"You, too, Steve," Gram said stiffly.

He gave Ginger another knuckle rub, this one more gentle. "See you, kiddo."

"Yeah, see you." Even when the front door slammed behind him, she couldn't believe he wouldn't stop Mom from loving Grant. Maybe next week he'd do something. Lots of kids at school said their fathers faded away after a divorce, but hers would never disappear like that.

"Want to keep the tube on?" Gram asked as they cleared the table.

"Okay, but I've got a book to read after we do the dishes." It struck her that no matter what *Incredible Journey* was about, it couldn't be worse than her life seemed now.

Gram rinsed the dishes. "You can't stop change, Ginger, even when it doesn't suit you. It's like when your grandfather died. It hurt me terribly, but I had to go on. You have to go on, no matter what your mother does."

Ginger loaded the dishwasher, not saying a thing. Mom had stenciled red hearts on the board over Gram's kitchen window, too. Yucky hearts and love everywhere. She hoped Mom wasn't letting Grant hold her hand . . . or kiss her!

"I hear Grant is a fine man," Gram said. "Your mother shouldn't have to be alone the rest of her life. He'll be good to her—"

Ginger closed her mind to Gram's words. She didn't know how she'd fight on, only that she couldn't give up. Green fingernails and trying to get Dad's help wouldn't be the half of it!

3

Ginger gazed out the car window as Mom drove. Sunday papers lay on the driveways and lawns; lots of people were still in bed. If only she were, too. Today she'd rather do anything than go to church and spend the afternoon at the Gabriels'.

Her mother hummed happily, making Ginger feel grouchier yet. "Why do I have to go to church just because you want to?" she asked. "It's not fair."

"We attend church because God wants us to," Mom replied. "If we love God, we enjoy going to church, too."

Crazy, Ginger thought. Besides, she didn't even know God. She'd never in her whole life seen Him or heard Him.

"In a way, loving God is like loving a person," her mother explained. "If you truly love someone, you want to spend special close times with him."

"Like you and Grant Gabriel?" Ginger asked, trying to change the subject—though neither subject was good.

"Yes, like Grant and me."

Mom began to hum again. After a while she said, "One of the good things about driving away from the beach in the morning is this sunshine."

Not even the morning sunshine raised Ginger's spirits. "Why are we going to his father's church?" she asked. "I'm not even used to Santa Rosita Community Church yet."

"We're attending out of courtesy to Grant's father," her mother said. "Dr. Gabriel was the minister there before he retired, and they asked him to preach today. I look forward to hearing him."

Ginger let out her breath slowly. "You'd think Grant would at least drive us there."

"It's out of his way. Besides, he has to dress Lilabet and help Joshua get breakfast. When you were only three like Lilabet, it took forever to get you ready to go anywhere. But it was worth it. You were darling, Ginger. Three year olds are so cute."

Yuck, Ginger thought. It didn't seem possible she'd ever been three—or darling. She slid a glance at her mother, who looked far too nice in the blue suit Gram had made for her. Why did Mom always have to look so nice lately?

Her mother patted Ginger's hand. "Don't worry, I'll never stop loving you—even if you do have green fingernails."

Ginger jerked her hand away. After awhile, she admired how well her fingernails matched her green-and-white flowery dress.

"Here we are," Mom announced as they drove into the church parking lot. "And, look, there's Grant and his children getting out of their car. There, in the next row."

Ginger saw Grant, then Joshua and Lilabet, coming around their car. She'd met his kids at Santa Rosita Community Church. Grant and Lilabet waved, but Joshua, who was eleven, eyed them with mistrust.

"Good morning," Grant called out. "What a nice picture the two of you make."

Her mother beamed. "And the three of you!"

Yuck, Ginger thought again. Lilabet did look cute, but Joshua didn't make such a good picture. He was trying to hold Lilabet's hand as she ran toward Mom. "Come on, hold hands," he said. "There are cars here. You'll get me in trouble."

Lilabet shook her head. Her straight blonde hair shone in the sunlight like a golden cap. "I don't wanna hold hands."

"Come on, Lilabet—"

As they neared, Ginger's mother asked, "May I hold your hand, Lilabet?"

Lilabet's brown eyes danced. "Yes."

30

Everyone smiled except Ginger. Sure Lilabet was cute, with her blonde hair and brown eyes, but Ginger wasn't going to let anyone know she thought so.

"What a beautiful yellow dress, Lilabet," Mom said. "With so many puffs and ruffles, you look like a flower."

Lilabet protested, "I'm not a flower!"

They all laughed, and even Ginger almost smiled.

Grant took Lilabet's other hand, and they led the way toward the big tan church, Mom's high heels clicking along on the sidewalk.

Ginger didn't like to see the three of them hold hands. Beside her, Joshua's usually friendly face turned grim, too. After a while he said, "Hey, green fingernails!"

"Yeah—so what?"

He smiled a little. "Maybe we can help each other out."

She glanced at him sideways. His brown hair was straight, like Lilabet's: sort of a bowl cut with long bangs, nicely done. "Are you planning to stick me with taking care of Lilabet?"

"Hey, maybe I should."

"Not me," Ginger answered.

"But that's not what I was thinking," he said.

Ginger decided not to ask. He could just tell her himself.

They walked along in silence until Lilabet called back, "You comin', Josh-wa?"

His face turned red. "We're comin', Lilabet."

31

"Why does she call you Josh-wa?"

He shrugged. "She just does. Lilabet has a funny way of saying things."

Ginger hid a grin. "Where'd she get that name, anyhow?"

"When she started talking, she couldn't say Elizabeth. Now we all call her Lilabet, too."

As they neared the church door, people greeted Grant, then glanced curiously at Ginger and her mother. Ginger tried to ignore them, scrutinizing her green fingernails instead.

"Let's find your Sunday school room," her mother said.

Now was the time to be bratty, Ginger decided. "I'm not going to Sunday school," she said. "I'm staying with you."

Her mother glanced at Grant.

"She can sit with us in church," he said. "Under the circumstances, that's probably best."

During the service, though, Ginger wished she were almost anywhere else. Sitting between Mom and Grant—caught in their lovesick glances—was worse than walking behind them and Lilabet. Ginger tried not to notice, and inspected the formal church instead. Dark wooden pews lined the sanctuary, stained-glass windows gleamed like jewels, and men wore suits with neckties.

Suddenly music burst from the organ, and gold-robed choir members marched up the aisle singing, "All hail the power of Jesus' name—"

32

"That's Grant's father," Mom whispered, nodding at the black-robed minister who followed the choir toward the pulpit.

The service continued, and Ginger sat back against the pew. Dr. Gabriel looked like Grant, except older and silvery haired. He sounded nice as he spoke, even if he did look sort of spooky in his black robe. Mostly he talked about love.

"Love is patient, love is kind," he said in his deep voice. "It does not envy, it does not boast, it is not proud. It is not rude, nor easily angered, it keeps no record of wrongs."

Ginger shrunk into herself. Maybe she wasn't good at love, but just look at what love was doing to Mom and Grant.

Dr. Gabriel ended, "The greatest is love."

He meant a different kind of love, Ginger guessed. Was there really a kind of love that came from loving God?

At last church was over, and people greeted each other.

Grant said, "This is Sallie and Ginger Trumbell," and everyone smiled at them.

One old lady said, "My dear, you have green fingernails!"

"They match my dress," Ginger answered.

"Indeed they do," the woman replied.

On the way to Grant's house, Ginger remembered Joshua's suggestion: *Maybe we can help each* other out. She'd take any help she could get.

Santa Rosita Hills was a long way inland from their own house near the beach. Here, it was warmer and bright with sunshine, and houses stood on sprawling green lawns, surrounded by flowers and trees. What would Grant's house look like? she wondered. She knew it had a pool, because he'd told them to bring their swimsuits. It bothered her that she didn't swim well, even if she did fool around in the ocean.

"Here we are," her mother said, driving into a shady lane of eucalyptus trees. "The Gabriels have only lived here two years. Grant and Dr. Gabriel sold their houses and bought this one after the accident. They haven't gotten around to all of the painting and repairs yet."

Ginger chewed her gum faster as she eyed the house. It was old and Spanish with arches in front. Great bursts of purple bougainvillea lay against the stucco walls, and red geraniums bloomed around the lawn.

"Isn't it charming?" Mom asked.

"I guess so," Ginger said.

As they climbed out of the car, a shaggy gray-and-white dog hurried out. "Woof!" he barked hoarsely. "Woof, woof!"

Mom said, "It's all right, Raffles."

"Woof yourself!" Ginger barked at the huge dog.

Her mother held a finger to her lips. "Shh! We don't want to awaken Lilabet from her nap."

Ginger drew an indignant breath.

Her mother ignored her and smiled at Raffles. "He's an old English sheepdog."

Big deal, Ginger thought. She snapped, "How do you know Lilabet's napping?"

"You mustn't be so jumpy. All three year olds take naps."

Ginger gave her gum a crack. She thought Mom would say, "Get rid of that gum right now!" but instead, she closed her eyes for an instant. Probably praying again.

Grant Gabriel opened the front door. He wore a white T-shirt and jeans, almost like her mother, who wore a white blouse with a denim skirt.

Had they planned to dress alike? Ginger wondered. Well, she'd almost worn a white shirt and jeans herself. A good thing she'd stuck with her brown T-shirt and brown shorts. Almost no one else ever wore all brown clothes.

"I thought I heard Raffles bark," Grant said. "He's usually our welcoming committee."

Raffles sat on the grass, panting. He stared at Ginger through hair so long and shaggy it covered his eyes. She could see his mouth, though, and it turned up as if he were smiling.

"Where's his tail?" Ginger asked.

"Old English sheepdogs don't have tails," Grant explained.

Raffles wagged his entire rear end as if he understood what Grant had said.

"He likes you, Ginger," Grant said.

Big deal! she thought again.

Grant smiled at her mother. "And I like you."

Her mother's face flushed happily. For an instant it looked like he wanted to kiss her, but she shook her head.

Ginger gave her gum a disgusted crack, and tucked towel, swimsuit, and book under her arm.

"Well," Grant said, "let's go around back."

The backyard was big, and flowers bloomed around the green lawn. The swimming pool was small and old, not like pools in movies or on TV. As they went through an iron gate, Ginger was glad to see a ping-pong table on the red tile patio—but not glad to see Joshua practicing.

"Your mom says you play a mean game of ping-pong," Grant said.

Ginger shrugged. "Yesterday I beat my father." The word "father" hung in the air even longer than she'd planned.

"Then you can probably beat me," Grant said, smiling.

If only I could make him mad, Ginger thought. She'd figure out something yet. Her eyes lit on Raffles, who was scratching his fleas. Maybe he offered possibilities.

"Hey, Ginger!" Joshua called from the ping-pong table. "How about a few games?"

"Sure," she answered. "Why not?"

He let down the other end of the table, and she

36

grabbed a paddle. She'd win, she told herself. And she'd win over Mom's romance with Grant Gabriel, too.

Joshua asked, "You want to rally for serve?"

"Sure. Let's see what you can do."

He was right-handed, she noticed. When he bounced the ball onto her side of the table, she slammed it to his left.

"Hey, you really can hit!"

Ginger served first, giving the ball so much spin his paddle fanned air. Her second serve slammed to his left corner again.

She beat him easily in all three games.

Joshua's brown eyes flashed. "You're good!"

"I practice a lot," she admitted.

Joshua grinned. "I'm best at soccer, I guess."

She could imagine him with that grin, holding a soccer ball under his arm like he was posed for a picture. She snapped out a decision. "I'm going to be on our school's soccer team next year."

"Oh, yeah? Where do you go to school?"

"Santa Rosita Elementary," she said. "I'm going into fifth grade."

Joshua said, "I'm going into sixth at Santa Rosita Christian."

"You mean where your dad's principal?" She couldn't imagine it. "You must have to be good."

Joshua shrugged and grinned again. "I should be, but Dad says I'm a long way from perfect. Hey, how about a swim?"

Ginger saw no way to get out of it. She looked for her mother and Grant, but they were gone, probably in the house.

"You can change in the guest room," Joshua said.

Before she knew what had happened, he had led her into the house and pointed her down a hallway. "Last room on the right. The yellow room."

The yellow room? Ginger swallowed hard, remembering her mother's words: "His guest room would look so beautiful with a white canopied bed. You'd be like a princess in it."

Behind her, Joshua said, "Come on out to the pool when you're ready."

"Sure."

She went down the hallway, and, hearing her mother's voice, stopped and peered into a room.

Her mother had just lifted Lilabet from her crib and was kissing the top of her blonde hair.

"I love you," Lilabet said.

Mom answered, "And I love you, Lilabet."

How could she! Ginger fumed. How could Mom do this? She didn't know who made her madder— Mom or Lilabet!

Before they could see her, Ginger hurried to the yellow bedroom and shut the door behind her. *Yuck*, she thought, *cheerful yellow*. A fluffy white rug covered most of the faded wood floor. She could imagine herself stuck in this room forever. It didn't help much that there were plain twin beds instead of a ruffled canopied bed. Her eyes fell on the cords

38

that held back white draperies over the window seat. Vroom, an idea hit.

Five minutes later, she stepped outside on the patio wearing her brown tank swimsuit. She carried *Incredible Journey*, in case things got too dull, and, wrapped in her towel, she carried a cord from the guest room drapes.

Raffles padded over, giving her another "Woof!"

"Hello, Raffles." As he waggled his rear end, she added, "Woof, woof!"

Joshua waited by the pool in his tan bathing suit. "Come on in, Ginger." He jumped into the water. "The water's warm."

Maybe if they talked it over, Joshua might help her stop Mom and Grant from getting more serious, Ginger thought, but she didn't know how to begin. Instead, she asked, "Are you allowed to swim if there's no one here?"

"You're here." He set off with a splash across the rippling blue water. When he stopped at the other side, he assured her, "Dad said it's okay. He can hear from the kitchen if you yell. Come on in."

She sat down next to the pool with Raffles. "I thought I'd read for a while."

Joshua's face fell with disappointment. "If that's what you want to do." He swam away toward the deep end, and Ginger opened her book.

Joshua swam and dove and splashed around for a long time while she pretended to read. After a while he yelled to her, "Hey, watch how long I can stay down on the bottom!"

"I'm watching," Ginger said and patted Raffles' head.

The moment Joshua dove, she whipped out the drapery cord. "Here, Raffles, sit and turn around a little."

As fast as she could, she tied his front feet together with the cord. It wasn't easy, but he was so big and dumb, he only licked her face with his rough tongue. His breath smelled awful. Finished, she sat back with her book and tried to look like she'd been reading all the while.

Joshua yelled, "Hey, how long was I under?"

Raffles jerked up, starting toward Joshua. Hindered by the cord around his feet, he yipped in panic and flopped sideways into the pool with a huge splash.

"Woof, woof, woof!" he barked wildly. He tried to paddle, but with his feet tied, he couldn't stay up.

"Dad!" Joshua yelled. "Dad! Help! Raffles can't swim!"

Aghast, Ginger stared at Raffles struggling in the water, then looked for a way to escape. She could hide by the old, overgrown guest house behind the pool.

Suddenly everyone ran out, and it was too late. Grant jumped into the pool, trying to get Raffles out. "Raffles, calm down!" he said. "Calm down!"

Raffles struck out in panic, clawing Grant's arms.

"Oh, Grant, you're cut!" Ginger's mother cried.

40

Lilabet yelled, "Daddy! Daddy! Get Raffles!"

After a fearful struggle, Grant dragged the huge dog from the water and onto the pool deck. Raffles lunged about slopping water, his feet still tied together.

"Who tied his feet?" Grant asked angrily, trying to untie them while Raffles struggled.

Joshua said, "Not me! I was swimming!"

Everyone's eyes turned to Ginger.

Her mother asked, "Ginger, did you do it?"

"Only for fun! I didn't mean for him to fall into the pool! Joshua yelled and the dog—"

"Never mind excuses," her mother said. "Look at the trouble you've caused. Grant's arms are bleeding, and Raffles almost drowned. Go sit in the car while we decide what to do with you."

Raffles shook himself wildly, flinging water all over and making Lilabet yell.

"To the car right now, Ginger!" her mother ordered.

Ginger grabbed her book and started for the car.

Her mother added, "If you think you've caused trouble so we can go home, you'd better think again."

Was that why she'd done it? Ginger wondered. If so, it hadn't worked out. On top of that, she felt awful about Raffles and about Grant's clothes being drenched. She didn't even want to think about his arms bleeding. Next time she wouldn't do anything so dumb.

41

4

Ginger sat in the car for a long time, chewing her gum and counting her aggravations. The main one was Mom falling in love and ruining everything. The next one was that Mom had no right to become a Christian and to change like she did.

The warm afternoon breeze blew through the open car windows; it fluttered the silvery green leaves on the eucalyptus trees. As Ginger sat there, she noticed the black iron "Gabriel" sign. *Hmmphh—Gabriel!* If it weren't for him, everything would still be all right.

She remembered Dr. Gabriel's sermon about love. "Love is patient, love is kind . . . it is not easily angered—" Well, what did that kind of stuff

matter? And what if Raffles did fall into the pool!
It'd drown his fleas anyhow.

"Ginger?" Grant said from outside the car window.

Ginger jumped in her seat.

"I'm sorry," he said. "I didn't mean to startle you.
Why don't we sit on the grass and talk?"

"No thanks!" she answered.

He shrugged lightly, and she saw he'd changed
into dry clothes. She darted a glance at his arms. At
least they'd stopped bleeding.

"I apologize for shouting at you, Ginger," he said.

"I guess I'm sorry for what I did to Raffles, too,"
she muttered. "I didn't know it would turn out so
. . . bad."

Grant's grayish-blue eyes met hers. "Sometimes
we don't know what troubles we set loose, even
when we don't mean to. I've done things like that
myself."

I'll bet, Ginger thought, looking away again.

"Another thing," he said, "I should have told you
how I feel about your mother. I'm afraid that's
what's really upsetting you."

Uh-oh! Ginger thought. Inside her mouth, she
stretched her gum in all directions with her tongue.

"I'm really not trying to steal your mother away,"
Grant explained. "That's not it at all. I want to
make her happy. And I know she loves you, so I'd
like to make you happy, too."

Hmmphh, Ginger thought. *Hmmphh.*

43

"I love Lilabet and Joshua very much," Grant continued. "Do you think your mother could steal me away from them?"

Yeah, Ginger thought. Mom probably could. And he could probably steal her mother from her, too. Anyone could see that from their lovesick looks.

"You know what I like about you, Ginger?" he asked.

"What?"

"I like how fiercely you love your mother and father. I even like your stubbornness. I'm stubborn sometimes myself."

She believed that.

"Come on," he urged, "let's go have a swim."

"I can't swim in a pool," she blurted. "I-I can only swim in the ocean."

"That's easily fixed," Grant replied. "I can teach you how to swim in the pool if you like."

"No thanks."

"The offer is always open." He paused. "Your mom says you like hamburgers. We'll be eating in an hour or so."

"I'm not hungry," Ginger replied, although just thinking about a big juicy hamburger made her almost drool.

"Well, maybe you can pretend we're friends and pretend to be hungry." He opened the car door. "May as well join us. Your mother won't be leaving anyhow. You can read your book."

Giving up, Ginger climbed out of the car. She'd

44

pretend they'd worked things out. It didn't mean she'd forgiven him or her mother for anything.

Passing the Gabriel sign, she asked, "What does Gabriel mean anyhow?"

"In the Bible, Gabriel is one of the archangels," Grant said. "That's a chief angel, one who's usually a messenger."

"Do you believe that stuff about angels?"

He let her in the gate. "I didn't always quite believe it, but now I do. There's a lot about the spiritual world we have to accept on faith."

She wanted to ask more, but Lilabet saw her. "Gin-ger! Gin-ger!" she yelled. She wore a yellow bathing suit with big white polka dots and a ruffle in back. She ran across the patio and flung herself at Ginger's legs.

"Hi, Lilabet," Ginger replied, her legs trapped in the little girl's grip.

Lilabet raised her big brown eyes. "Hold me?"

Ginger didn't see any way out of it. "Okay."

Grant started toward the pool. "There's chips and dip on the patio table. Help yourselves."

Ginger nodded, lifting Lilabet into her arms.

"I love you, Gin-ger," Lilabet said.

Something softened in Ginger's heart, and she held Lilabet's cheek against her own.

Ever so sweetly, Lilabet asked, "Do you love me?"

Ginger swallowed hard. "Come on, Lilabet. Let's go get some chips."

45

Lilabet patted Ginger's curls. "You have pretty hair."

"You're crazy," Ginger muttered. She'd give anything to have blonde hair like Lilabet's or brown hair like Grant's and Joshua's. Even Raffles' hair wasn't as curly as hers. It was still damp as he lay there asleep in the sunshine.

Mom was swimming across the pool like nothing had gone wrong, and now Grant dove in. On the patio by the house Joshua yelled, "Hey, Ginger, how about another game of ping-pong?"

"Play with me, Gin-ger," Lilabet begged, wiggling down so she could get her beat-up bear puppet.

It might not be such a bad afternoon after all, Ginger thought and started for the dip and chips.

Later, she beat Joshua in another three games of ping-pong. No sense in letting him beat her, she'd decided. Joshua probably wouldn't help her stop the romance anyhow, not after she'd almost drowned his dog.

When they'd finished playing ping-pong, her mom was at work in the kitchen. She called from the window, "Would you two set the patio table for dinner?"

"Sure," Ginger answered, glad she didn't mention Raffles' dunk in the pool. Maybe nobody would.

She and Joshua spread a red-and-white checkered cloth over the table, then brought out silverware, paper plates, and cups. Lilabet said importantly,

46

"I can help." She put paper napkins under the forks without making too much of a mess, and Grant cooked thick hamburger patties on the barbecue grill.

"Here comes Grandfather Gabriel!" Joshua said. "Just in time for supper."

Joshua's grandfather laughed. "Good timing, as usual."

He looked different in a red and tan plaid shirt and tan pants, Ginger thought. He had a nice sparkle in his gray-blue eyes, but she'd noticed that this morning, even when he wore his black minister's robe.

"Ginger, I'm glad to see you," he said.

"Hello," she answered. She wasn't sure what to call him, but she added, "Dr. Gabriel."

"Most young people call me Grandfather Gabriel. I'd be pleased if you would, too," he said with a grin. "What shall I call you—Ginger, or is it Virginia?"

"My real name is Virginia—"

"Shall I call you Virginia then?" he asked.

No one ever had, and she liked the grown-up way Virginia sounded when he pronounced it. "You can, but nobody else."

"I'm honored," he said. "Virginia it is."

"Grandfather's been to the baseball game," Joshua said.

"To the baseball game?" she asked.

"He has a season ticket," Joshua explained.

47

"You do?" Ginger asked, a little surprised.

Grandfather Gabriel laughed. "I do. And I yell."

"You yell?" She couldn't imagine a minister yelling at a ball game or anywhere else.

He nodded, still smiling. "I'm an enthusiastic fan."

"He played professional baseball for three years," Joshua explained. "He was a really good pitcher, but he wanted to be a minister instead."

Ginger couldn't imagine giving up pitching to be a minister. It sounded crazy.

As if guessing her thoughts, he said, "Now don't go making anything too special of me. Ministers aren't perfect, either."

"No?" For some reason she thought ministers —and all Christians—were supposed to be perfect. Not that Mom was yet . . . and Grant had lost his temper about Raffles' legs being tied together.

"No," Grandfather Gabriel answered, amused. Just then Raffles ambled over and rubbed against his leg. "Raffles, how did you get wet? Did you fall into the pool again?"

Raffles eyed Ginger warily, and she felt her face redden.

Grandfather Gabriel raised a curious brow, glancing from her to Joshua, then quickly said, "Raffles was already grown when he was given to us, so we thought he might be sensible. Unfortunately, the very first thing he did was walk right into the pool's deep end."

48

Joshua added, "And the first thing you did was trim the hair hanging over his eyes."

Grandfather shook his head at Raffles and laughed. "He's lovable, but not too sensible."

Her mother placed food on the kitchen window pass-through. "Here are things for the table."

"Don't let me keep you two from your work," Grandfather Gabriel said. "I'll get Lilabet away from the chips and dip. Look at her gobbling them up."

Relieved that he hadn't learned about Raffles' dunk in the pool, Ginger helped Joshua put the food on the table.

At supper, she sat between her mother and Joshua. Lilabet sat between Mom and Grant, potato chip crumbs around her mouth. "Oh boy, hamburgers!" she crowed. She wore a pink-and-white striped pinafore that Ginger's mother called "precious."

Grant chuckled. "Lilabet, you sound like you haven't eaten for a week. Let's hope I made enough to fill you up."

"She's always hungry," Joshua remarked to Ginger. "But at least she doesn't bite me anymore."

"You mean she used to?" Ginger asked.

"Did she! She bit everyone when she was teething."

Grandfather Gabriel said, "Wait a minute, Lilabet, until we sing grace."

Before Ginger knew what had happened, they all

49

held hands, and she didn't see how she could let loose of Joshua's or her mother's. The others sang in the warm summer breeze:

"Praise God from whom all blessings flow,
Praise Him all creatures here below,
Praise Him above, Ye heavenly host,
Praise Father, Son, and Holy Ghost."

She felt stupid, not knowing the words, and she wondered if the neighbors heard them singing. Well, they were probably used to it, living next door to a minister.

Grant said to Ginger's mother, "What a beautiful day."

"Yes," she agreed. "Almost perfect."

Ginger guessed that meant she hadn't ruined it for them. Anyhow Raffles was fine, even if he did keep his distance. She spread mustard, ketchup, and mayonnaise on a bun, centered a meat patty and a tomato slice on one side, and put it together. It barely fit into her mouth, but it tasted w-o-n-d-e-r-f-u-l.

Beside her, Mom smiled happily. Right over Lilabet's head, Mom and Grant exchanged a gooey look.

Joshua whispered, "Think they'll break the big news now?"

"What big news?" Ginger asked.

"You know, that they're going to get married."

No! Ginger thought. *No! Mom will never marry him! If anything, she'll marry Dad again!*

Ginger glanced at them again, and her heart sank. They were holding hands behind Lilabet.

Grant asked, "Should we tell them now?"

"I don't know," her mother replied, dimpling a little.

Suddenly Ginger said in her loudest voice, "I feel sick!" She nearly knocked her chair over as she pushed away from the table and ran wildly to the car. Joshua was right about what they planned to announce—and she didn't want to hear a word of it!

5

"Ginger, time to wake up," her mother said at the bedroom door. "It's Monday. I have to go to work."

Ginger rolled over, then slowly made herself sit up in bed. Yesterday's awful scene at the Gabriels' flew to mind at once. Had she really jumped up from the table and yelled, "I'm sick!"?

And had she really been sick to her stomach in the geraniums on the way to the car? Only Mom had seen that disgusting sight, but instead of soothing her, she'd said, "I'm afraid you've brought this on yourself."

Now Mom stepped into her room. "Do you feel all right?"

"I guess so," Ginger replied. She avoided her

mother's gaze and eyed her stuffed animal collection: Parrot, Spider, Octopus, Dinosaur, and Fish. Most of them were weird, like her.

"Good," Mom said. "Please hurry. You can wash at Gram's house. I'm driving across town to Santa Rosita Legal Services. I've taken another temporary job."

Ginger pulled on a clean white T-shirt and her old brown shorts, and grabbed Parrot. Unwrapping a stick of gum, she stuck it into her mouth and began to chew.

Outside, the morning cloud bank still hid the sun. As they climbed into the car, Ginger suddenly wondered if her mother were hiding something. What if she were only pretending to love Grant Gabriel? "Mom," she said, "do you like Grant because he has lots of money?"

Her mother laughed as she started the car. "You think I like Grant because he has money?"

"I just wondered," Ginger said stiffly. She looked out the window at the houses and palm trees lining the street.

"I like him because he's a fine man," her mother answered. "He's one of the finest people I've ever met. Why do you ask?"

"I thought maybe, if we needed more money, I could baby-sit and maybe deliver the Santa Rosita paper."

Her mother patted her hand. "I appreciate your thoughtfulness, Ginger, but let's hold off on your working for a while. I promise I don't like Grant for his money. Anyhow, he's not rich."

"He's not?" Ginger asked.

"No," Mom said. "He was a teacher, and summers he worked in real estate. After his wife and his mother died in the accident, he and Grandfather sold their houses and moved into this one. Grant went back to school, then took the job at Santa Rosita Christian. Didn't I tell you all that before?"

"Yeah. I guess I forgot."

After a moment Mom added, "Grandfather Gabriel was hurt badly in the accident, too. It's a miracle he's alive."

They drove up in front of Gram's house, and sat there, looking at each other. Mom said, "They're making a new life, Ginger, just as we've done in the past few years."

"Then we'd better not ruin it!" Ginger almost snapped.

Mom answered, "We're putting that in God's hands."

Ginger looked away. If only she didn't feel so guilty! Even though Mom had told her a hundred times the divorce had nothing to do with her, she still felt responsible.

"I'd better get going," Mom said. "Please tell Gram I'm not working tomorrow afternoon. We're going to the beach with Grant and the children."

"Do we have to?" Ginger asked.

"I've accepted his invitation for both of us."

Yuck, Ginger thought and let herself out of the car. Maybe Gram could get her out of going to the beach with them.

"Have a nice day, dear!" her mother called after her.

At least at Gram's everything will be normal, she thought as she hurried up the cracked sidewalk to the old white house. She didn't need one more thing to change.

The front door was already unlocked, and Ginger let herself in. "It's me, Gram," she announced.

"I'm on the phone," her grandmother called, so Ginger ambled into the kitchen.

Still on the phone, Gram gave her a little wave and asked, "Do you know if your mother's working tomorrow afternoon?"

"She's off."

"Good." Gram turned and spoke into the phone. "I'd be glad to go with you to the senior center, Alice."

Ginger's spirits drooped. Now she'd have to go to the beach with Mom and the Gabriels.

The next afternoon, Ginger and her mother quickly cleaned the house. "I don't know why it has to be so perfect," Ginger grumbled. "Grant's been here plenty of times."

"Joshua and Lilabet haven't," her mother returned. "Do you want them to think we're slobs?"

Ginger whisked a rag between the magazines on

the coffee table. "I don't think they'll notice whether it's clean or not."

"That's not the point, Ginger. Dust the magazines, too."

Ginger gave the magazines a fast swipe. A good thing Lilabet still took naps, so they couldn't come until she woke up. "Anyhow," she said, "why are they coming here first?"

"You know parking at the beach is impossible," Mom said. "It's easier to walk from here."

Vroom! An idea hit. Mom had iced tea in the refrigerator. Grant would probably drink iced tea.

The minute Mom left for her bedroom to change clothes, Ginger hurried to the kitchen and poured salt into the sugar bowl. When Grant got a mouthful of that, he'd know she didn't want him coming around here.

At three-thirty, Ginger was already in her swimsuit when she saw him park his car under her favorite palm tree. "They're here!"

"Why don't you run a comb through your hair?" Mom said.

"Because I can't get a comb through it!"

"You know what I mean. Brush it. And don't be sassy."

Glad to escape, Ginger hurried off. In her bedroom, she peered into the mirror. Her freckles were dark as ever, her eyes still cat green. Her wild hair curled up like copper shavings in the metal shop where Mom had once worked as a secretary. Backing away from the mirror, Ginger brushed her hair hard. It was still awful hair. And one other thing wasn't changing, she thought as she stood there in her bathing suit: she was still straight up and down.

Her mother called out, "Ginger, everyone's here."

"Coming," Ginger answered. She couldn't wait to see if Grant had salted his iced tea. Wouldn't he choke!

Lilabet peeked at her from the hallway, clutching an old rag doll. "Gin-ger!" she crowed. Lilabet ran straight for her, grabbing her legs again. "Gin-ger! Gin-ger!"

"Hi, Lilabet," Ginger said. She tried to pry the little fingers from her legs. "Hey, let go!"

Lilabet raised her arms. "Carry me, please?"

"Why not?" Ginger lifted her up, and Lilabet wound her legs around her waist.

In the kitchen, she found Joshua and Grant with her mother, eating cookies and drinking lemonade. Lemonade! He hadn't touched the salt in the sugar bowl!

Trying to look innocent, Ginger exchanged greetings with him and Joshua. She turned to Mom. "Where's the iced tea?"

"It was old, so I threw it out," her mother answered.

Uff! Ginger thought. Well, she'd make him mad yet.

Grant said, "Sallie, I'm serious about you stenciling hearts and flowers around the border of

Lilabet's bedroom ceiling. I'd be happy to pay you. It's the one room we painted and had newly carpeted before we moved into the house."

"I'd love to do it for Lilabet," Mom replied, "but I wouldn't dream of accepting a penny for it."

Yuck, Ginger said to herself. She grabbed a chocolate chip cookie from the tray on the counter.

"No gingersnaps?" Joshua asked with a grin. "I thought you'd only eat *ginger*snaps and drink *ginger* ale."

"Bad joke," she snapped at him.

Lilabet slid down from Ginger and shook her finger at him. "Josh-wa is bad!"

Grant didn't quite hide a grin. "Lilabet brings the truth to light, as usual. I told them you don't appreciate gingersnap jokes, but I guess Joshua couldn't resist."

"Sorry," Joshua apologized, though he grinned a bit, too.

Ginger said, "It's all right. I'm used to them anyhow." No sense in letting Joshua get the better of her, she decided. Besides, he had said, "Maybe we can help each other out." Maybe they still could. She hadn't given him much of a chance Sunday with her nearly drowning Raffles.

"I've packed a picnic lunch in the cooler," Mom said. "And there's a big thermos of lemonade in the fridge. Maybe I should take Lilabet to the bathroom."

Lilabet announced it, "I'm going potty."

Joshua rolled his eyes toward the ceiling.

His father suggested, "Let's get our towels and things from the car, Josh."

At last they locked the house and started down the street toward Ocean Avenue in the afternoon sunshine. Lilabet held her father's hand on one side; on the other, she held her rag doll, Raggy, for Mom to hold. Ginger tried to ignore the cozy picture they made. She and Joshua struggled along behind, carrying the cooler between them. Her other arm was full of beach towels, and Lilabet's yellow plastic pail dangled from her fingertips.

"I brought a Frisbee and a volleyball," Joshua said, "since you're so good at sports."

"Great. I'm going to be on the volleyball team at school," she bragged, then wondered if her school even had a volleyball team.

They crossed Ocean Avenue at the stoplight, then started down the steep sandy path to the beach. The rackety rumble of cars and trucks faded, replaced by the wonderful thundering of the ocean. Overhead, the sun shone brightly, and the ocean shimmered a silvery blue as far as she could see.

"Do you come here a lot?" Joshua asked.

"Almost every day with Gram. We used to come with my best friend, Mandy Timmons, but she just moved to Chicago," Ginger said, then regretted it. Just the thought of Mandy being gone made her heart hurt.

"You'd probably miss it if you moved," he said.

59

"I sure would," Ginger answered emphatically.

Joshua frowned as if he knew something unpleasant, but she decided not to ask. Instead, she inhaled the salty ocean air and eyed the beach for shells for her collection.

They spread their beach towels and old blankets on the hot sand, not far from where the waves crashed to the shore.

Ginger's mother warned, "Don't go out too far, Ginger."

"I won't," Ginger said, embarrassed. It was bad enough that she couldn't swim without her mother making an issue of it. Besides, she'd told Grant she could swim in the ocean.

Lilabet gave her rag doll to Ginger, "Raggy wants to swim."

"No, Lilabet," Joshua said with a laugh. "I guess she remembers Raffles' dunking in the pool yesterday."

Heat rushed up Ginger's face, and she kicked up a spray of dry sand. Turning toward her mother and Grant, she felt even worse.

Mom had taken off her white terry beach cover-up. She was beautiful in her blue swimsuit, and her dimples deepened as she talked to Grant. He wasn't as muscular as Dad was from surfing, but he had broader shoulders. They looked too nice together, Ginger thought. Worse, they looked as if they belonged to each other and not to the rest of them. They reached for each other's hands.

Ginger shouted, "Let's swim!" She dashed across the sand to the thundering surf and splashed in.

The water swirled around her feet, then waves rushed against her legs. She splashed onward through gentle swells until the water was over her waist, but she pushed on and on. Her mother called out over the ocean's roar, and Grant yelled.

Anger drove Ginger forward. *I'll show them*, she thought. *I'll make them sorry!*

The waves rose higher and higher, breaking and slamming against her as they raced toward the beach. Suddenly a mountainous wave rushed at her. Before she could yell, it lifted her toward the sky's blueness, then pulled her down with its crashing force. It somersaulted her through the water, and her knees scraped against the rough ocean bottom.

As she surfaced, she cried out "Help!" and choked on a mouthful of salt water. Another wave tumbled her and pulled her under, then another and another. "Help!" Pitching and plunging through the dark water, she floundered in terror.

Someone grabbed her arm, jerking her upright.

"Help!" she screamed, choking on salt water again. She clawed wildly at the man's shoulders.

"It's all right, Ginger!" Grant shouted over the ocean's roar. "You'll be all right now."

Another wave rushed at them, and she clawed him again. He pulled away.

"Stop that, Ginger!" he ordered. Then he said, "I'll hold my hand out to you. You must be calm."

61

She grabbed his hand wildly. Another wave rushed at them, and he held her alongside him as they rose up with it.

"I can take care of you," he told her. "Calm, now, calm." His words relaxed her a little, and the oncoming wave wasn't as frightening. He half held, half carried her. "Let's head for shore."

He set her down at last, and she was relieved to feel her feet touch the sandy bottom. Finally there were just gentle swells, and they walked through them together.

Pale with worry, Mom held Lilabet's hand at the water's edge, where Joshua stood beside them. Mom called out, "Are you all right, Ginger?"

"Oh, Mom—" Splashing through the water, Ginger threw herself into her mother's arms.

"Ginger, oh, Ginger!" Mom cried.

"I'm sorry. I'll never go so far out again!" Ginger promised against her mother's shoulder. To her horror, hot tears spilled from her eyes.

Mom said, "I've told you, you have to learn how to swim!"

A lifeguard appeared beside them. "You all right?"

Ginger nodded, backhanding the tears from her eyes.

"Good." He turned to Grant. "I just finished a rescue farther out. A good thing you knew what to do." He paused. "Say, you're scratched. Better come get some ointment."

Ginger's heart sank as she saw the fresh scratches on Grant's shoulders. Sunday she'd caused Raffles to fall into the pool and scratch Grant—and now today she'd scratched him herself. She made herself say, "I'm sorry, Grant."

"You're worth it," he answered. He ruffled her wet hair, but it wasn't a knuckle rub. "If I had to, I'd rescue you all over again."

Lilabet spoke solemnly. "Daddy loves Gin-ger."

"I sure do," he agreed. "I sure do."

Fresh tears clouded Ginger's eyes. She was grateful that he'd saved her life, but she didn't love him! She was sorry as she could be that she'd caused so much trouble, but the truth was that she didn't love a single one of the Gabriels!

6

The next morning Mom almost choked on her cereal. She coughed it out into her napkin, then ran to the sink for a glass of water. After drinking, she asked, "Ginger Anne Trumbell, did you put salt in the sugar bowl?"

"I didn't mean for you to get it!" Ginger said.

Mom took another drink, then leaned weakly against the sink. "Who, may I ask, was supposed to get a mouthful of salt instead of sugar? Grant?"

Ginger stared at her orange juice. "I thought he'd have iced tea. That was before we went to the beach and—"

"And he saved you," Mom finished for her, a gaggy look still on her face. "I see. Please, Ginger, let's not have any more dumb tricks."

"Okay," Ginger agreed unhappily.

"And don't look so glum," her mother added. "I'm the wronged party, not you. Now let's see if we can't cheer up. We have a whole day ahead of us."

Ginger forced a small smile.

The morning didn't improve. Mom must have phoned Gram the night before, because the minute Ginger walked into the house Gram said, "I hear you nearly drowned."

"Yeah, I guess so."

Gram gave her an astonished look. "You guess so! Is that all you can say about it?"

Ginger shrugged. "I don't want to talk about it."

"Well, I can't say I blame you," Gram said, "but I do want to tell you I'm grateful to Grant Gabriel. You're the best granddaughter I've ever had."

"I'm the only one," Ginger pointed out.

"Well, I love you like you're the best anyone ever had," Gram stated and gave her a hug. "Let's have breakfast. And I don't care if you already ate."

In the kitchen, Gram took freshly baked blueberry muffins from the oven. "Where's your mom working now? I lose track."

"Santa Rosita Legal Services," Ginger told her and began to set the table.

Gram put the hot muffins into a basket. "Permanent work?"

Ginger shook her head. "Just for six weeks."

"I wonder why she doesn't take a permanent job with them," Gram mused. "They're always after her to. But then, so are most of the companies she works for."

It was nice that Mom's employers liked her, Ginger thought, but this morning Mom had said something unnerving. "She's not working the last half of August."

"Oh, really?" Gram responded with interest. "Well, your mother's never been what you might call 'a career woman.' She can take work or leave it. Personally I think Grant Gabriel is right, that she has a flair for decorating. I'm glad he's encouraging her to take classes. I've worked at a nine-to-five job myself and, for most people, 'career' is just a fancy word for 'work.'"

"Mom sure did like working for Grant," Ginger grumbled. He and Santa Rosita Christian School had turned her into a Christian, even if Mom claimed the Holy Spirit did it.

After breakfast, Ginger headed out to the front porch with a pen and the stationery Gram had given her for her birthday. Sitting down on the swing, she took out a sheet of yellow paper. On top was a picture that looked like Parrot. His open mouth squawked: HERE'S THE LATEST FROM GINGER ANNE TRUMBELL!

Dear Mandy, she wrote,
I miss you. I read Incredible Journey, *and it made me think of you moving*

66

away. Sad, very sad. Can you imagine those dogs and the cat traveling like that?

It's still foggy June weather. I've only seen a few kids from school at the beach. Mom says there aren't enough kids in the neighborhood anymore.

Lots is new here. Remember how I worried about Mom dating Grant Gabriel? Well, it's gotten worse. Last Sunday we went to his father's church to hear him preach. In the afternoon we had to go to their house. He has two kids. Joshua is eleven, and Lilabet is three. As usual, I snapped and made a mess of things.

Tuesday we went to the beach with them. I nearly drowned, and Grant saved me. Now I feel even worse. I have to go to a church youth group with them tonight. I don't want to go! I hate getting our families together. Why can't everything stay the same like last summer when you were still here?

Anyhow, thanks for Incredible Journey. *Parrot and I are going to read it again now and think of you.*

Your forever friend,
Ginger

That evening Grant drove them to Santa Rosita Community Church. Luckily Lilabet sat in a car seat between her and Joshua and she talked a lot. When she saw the church she sang loudly, *"Jesus loves me, this I know . . ."*

Joshua made a discouraged face. "Lilabet, not so loud."

Lilabet sang even louder, getting the words all tangled.

Grant said with a laugh, "We love your singing, Lilabet, but other people like to talk. Why don't you wait until you're in class? They'll have lots of good songs to sing."

Ginger asked, "You mean Lilabet has a class to go to?"

"We all do," her mother replied. "You'll enjoy it."

Ginger didn't think so. But if even Lilabet had to go to class, she couldn't complain.

Community Church, as everyone called it, had new white buildings and new spindly trees. Red geraniums bloomed around the bright green lawn. Ginger had only attended a few Sunday services with her mother, but this church felt more familiar and casual than Grandfather Gabriel's. People didn't dress up so much, and the pastor didn't wear a robe.

As they walked up the sidewalk, Joshua joined his friends, and Ginger grew more nervous. When they reached the classrooms out back, Lilabet sang louder than ever, *"Jesus loves me . . ."*

"Here you are, Ginger," Grant said. "This is Miss Birmingham, our fifth-grade teacher."

Miss Birmingham had short dark curls and big green eyes the same shade as Ginger's. She wore a blue denim skirt like Ginger's too, and a white T-shirt that said *Good News Club*. She smiled. "We're pleased to have you join us, Ginger. Won't you come meet the other girls?"

Before Ginger knew it, she was in a classroom full of chattering girls. She recognized a few from school. Everyone wore Good News Club T-shirts except her.

Miss Birmingham handed her a pink name tag shaped like a shell. "We're the pink shells."

Yuck, pink, Ginger thought. Pink was for sweety-sweet girls, not girls like her. The only good thing was the tag's shape, which reminded her of a shell in her collection.

Miss Birmingham called out, "Katie, would you help our visitor feel welcome here at Good News Club?"

Ginger dreaded to see who Katie might be.

"This is Katie Cameron," Miss Birmingham said.

To her surprise, Ginger was pleased. Katie had plain brown hair, straight and tied into a pony-tail—exactly the color of hair Ginger wished for herself. Freckles covered Katie's nose and her brown eyes sparkled.

"Hey, Ginger," Katie said with a friendly smile. "I'm new here, too. I've just lived in Santa Rosita for a few weeks. Where do you come from?"

Ginger bristled. "I've lived here all of my life! It's

just the first time I've had to come to a youth meeting."

"Oh," Katie replied, embarrassed.

"I guess you wouldn't know," Ginger said.

"I surely didn't," Katie answered. "We just moved here from Georgia."

"Oh. I thought you sounded different," Ginger said. It was hard to understand her.

"Everybody teases us about talking southern," Katie told her, "but we truly can't help it."

"I guess not," Ginger said. "Maybe you'll get over it."

"I don't know," Katie answered with a smile and a little shake of her head. "Anyhow, let's go sit in the chair circle. That's where we started last week." She smiled again as if she didn't mind getting stuck with Ginger.

Katie added, "I saw you come to church with the Gabriels. They're my neighbors. Last week they let me stay with Lilabet while she was napping."

"You baby-sat Lilabet?" Ginger asked.

"Only while she slept. They said when I'm older, I can really baby-sit. I'm just ten."

"Me too," Ginger replied. She felt more comfortable, even though she considered herself as going on eleven. It popped into her head to ask, "Have you ever heard Lilabet sing?"

"Hey, have I ever!" Katie laughed. "Isn't she fun?"

"I guess I'm . . . not so sure yet."

70

As they talked, Katie put in so many "heys" and "y'alls" and "Ah'll be doggeds" that Ginger couldn't help being interested. After a while, she got more used to Katie's southern talk and didn't have to strain to understand her.

Before long, all of the class sat in the circle of chairs, and Miss Birmingham clapped for attention. "Let's begin with song 37, 'Michael, Row the Boat Ashore,' " she said, strapping a guitar around her neck and strumming a chord.

Ginger thumbed through the songbook to 37, then sang with the rest of them. It didn't make sense about rowing the boat ashore, but everyone seemed to like it.

"Now let's sing song 59, 'Jacob's Ladder,' " Miss Birmingham suggested.

It made even less sense than singing about Michael. A note under the song said, "Climbing Jacob's Ladder means living, climbing through life with God to help us."

Miss Birmingham made announcements about summer camp and roller-skating and a trip to Disneyland.

Katie whispered, "Maybe you could go to camp."

"I don't think so," Ginger answered. She wasn't going to any summer camp! She couldn't roller-skate well either, but she'd sure like to go to Disneyland again.

Next they gave points for bringing Bibles and wearing Good News Club T-shirts. Everyone

71

received a point for attendance. Miss Birmingham asked, "And now, who knows today's Bible verse?"

One of the girls said, "Galatians 5:22. 'But the fruit of the Spirit is love, joy, peace, patience, kindness, goodness, faithfulness, gentleness and self-control.' "

Ginger decided she didn't have much of any of them. Probably Katie did. She asked her, "What are the points for?"

"If we get enough, we get Disneyland tickets," Katie explained. "I probably can't go. I haven't lived here long enough to get that many points."

"Now let's have another song," Miss Birmingham announced. "How about 'We Are One in the Spirit'? Song 73."

It must mean the Holy Spirit, Ginger decided.

After they finished singing, Miss Birmingham said, "One of the most wonderful things about Jesus is He's an always-there, always-loving friend. If there is anyone here who would like to have Jesus as her friend, you can pray with me now. Or, if you already know Him, you might want to pray about spending more time with Him." She led a prayer, but Ginger didn't pay much attention to it.

Miss Birmingham announced, "Relay races outside on the playground. Pink shells play the yellow shells."

"I haven't been in a relay race since school's been out," Ginger told Katie excitedly as they hurried outside.

72

"Hey, you must like sports," Katie laughed.

"I'm the best in my class at Santa Rosita Elementary," Ginger said, then realized it sounded like bragging.

Outside, she threw herself into the relay races. The best was a clown relay. She pulled a baggy red clown suit over her clothes, ran to a stake, stripped the suit off, and raced back.

"Come on, pink shells!" her team yelled. "Come on, Ginger!" The pink shells won all four relays because she was so fast.

Going to the Good News Club wasn't so bad after all, Ginger decided. If she had to go again, though, Mom was going to have to buy her a club T-shirt. The only trouble was that stuff about being full of love, joy, peace, kindness, and all. She stuck a fresh stick of gum into her mouth and chewed hard and fast.

When the meeting ended, Ginger saw Mom and Grant stroll up the sidewalk toward her against a golden sunset. They smiled at each other, holding Lilabet's hands between them.

Ginger gave her gum a loud, worried crack.

As if she didn't have enough troubles, Mom probably thought she should be kind and loving and the rest of it now. But how could she be all those when, just seeing Mom and Grant and Lilabet together, she felt so mad and jealous?

7

Saturday afternoon Ginger and her mother drove to the Gabriels' house again. Mom waved her hand in front of Ginger's face. "Are you there, Ginger Trumbell?"

Ginger shook her head. "I was thinking."

Actually, she was wishing she could speak to Dad today, but he'd stayed up north to surf with friends. It seemed that only she cared about stopping the romance between Mom and Grant. Heaving a sigh, Ginger climbed out of the car.

Mom called out, "Here comes Raffles!"

Sure enough, Raffles loped toward them from the front door, a shaggy blimp on legs. He stopped in front of Ginger and peered at her through his long hair. Did he remember she'd almost drowned him? It didn't look like it, since he was smiling and wagging his rear end.

And here came Grant. Oh, no . . . he was going to kiss Mom! Ginger turned to Raffles. Stalling for time, she ran her hand over his shaggy coat and said, "You're a funny dog."

Raffles licked her face with his warm, rough tongue and wagged his rear end harder than ever. His doggy breath was still awful. Next, she guessed, he'd sit back down and scratch his fleas. Sure enough, he did.

Behind her, Grant said to Ginger's mother, "Lilabet's about to wake up. You can start stenciling in her room now, if you still want to."

"I can't wait to begin," Mom said.

The plan was for her to stencil a border of lavender hearts and flowers around Lilabet's ceiling. In return, Grant would give Ginger swimming lessons. He'd even promised to make dinner. This morning, Ginger had argued fiercely against swimming lessons, but her mother wouldn't budge.

"Ginger," she'd said, "I love you so much that you have to learn to swim. I can't risk losing you! What's more, I love Grant, and he loves me. Please try to like him and his family."

"I don't want to!" Ginger answered. "I don't want to!"

Instead of arguing, Mom had closed her eyes as if in prayer again.

In the house, the smell of simmering spaghetti sauce filled the air. Ginger asked Grant, "Do you always cook?"

He chuckled. "Afraid not. Our housekeeper, Maria, has done most of our cooking for the past three years."

Ever since the accident, Ginger thought. Mom said Maria took care of Lilabet, too, except on weekends.

"Katie's out back," Grant said. "She wants a swimming lesson, too."

Planned. He and Mom had planned that, Ginger guessed.

"Joshua's at a baseball game," Grant said.

Planned for sure, Ginger decided. She heard Lilabet singing loudly upstairs in her room. "I'll go out back," Ginger announced.

"You could put on your bathing suit," her mother said.

"I wore it under my clothes." Anything to avoid the yellow guest room and thoughts of a canopied bed. She hurried to the kitchen door.

Raffles followed her out onto the patio, where Katie lay on a lounge reading a book. She wore a blue tank suit, and Ginger was glad to see that she was still straight up and down, too.

"Hey, Ginger!" Katie sat up, looking pleased to see her.

"Hi. I bet you can already swim."

Katie shook her head, her brown ponytail

76

swishing back and forth in the sunshine. "I can barely float, but I surely do want to learn."

"I guess I will too, then," Ginger decided. "I go out in the ocean a lot, but I've never been around pools much." Hopefully Katie hadn't heard about her almost drowning in the ocean three days ago. Ginger stripped down to her brown tank suit, determined to learn to swim faster than Katie. "You know what?" she asked.

"What?" Katie answered.

"Either you're talking better, or I'm getting used to your southern accent."

Katie laughed.

Grant arrived, wearing his red swim trunks. "Looks like you're both ready. You can remember this as the day you really began to swim. Let's get in the water and try bobbing."

"I can do that!" Ginger snapped.

"Good," Grant said. "I'm glad to hear it."

Katie rippled the water with her hands. "It's warm. It surely does feel good."

Ginger splashed water at her, and Katie laughed.

All through their lesson, Raffles paced alongside the pool. An hour later, Ginger still didn't know how to swim, but she could bob and hold onto the edge of the pool while she kicked. She'd even learned to float. But it seemed she had to work ten times harder than Katie to keep up.

"Good job, girls," Grant said as they climbed out of the pool. "Say, want to stay for dinner, Katie?"

77

Katie asked Ginger. "Would you like me to?"

"Yeah, I guess so."

"Good," Grant said. "I'll phone your mother. And I'd better see how our artist is doing, too. She must be keeping Lilabet entertained with the stenciling."

After he'd gone in, Katie remarked, "The Gabriels are such a nice family. I surely am glad we moved next door to them."

"Where are you going to school?" Ginger asked.

Katie's smile reached all the way to her brown eyes. "Santa Rosita Christian. I went to a Christian school in Georgia—and then we moved here, right next to the principal of the Christian school! We didn't even know it till after we moved in. Dad says we were led."

Uff. Katie talked Christian, like Mom did now, and like Grant. Before Katie could get any more Christian, Ginger asked, "Do you like living here?"

Katie nodded. "I like the weather and the way it doesn't get humid in the summer. But I surely do miss my cousins and other relatives."

Raffles glanced back and forth at them while they visited. He looked pleased, too, that Katie got to stay for dinner.

When Grandfather Gabriel brought Joshua home, they all sat down to eat out on the patio. This time Grant prayed. "Father, You have told us in Scripture that where two or three of us are gathered in Your name, You will be in the midst of us."

Does he really think God is here in the middle of us? Ginger wondered. She scarcely heard the rest.

Dinner was all right though: salad, garlic bread, and d-e-l-i-c-i-o-u-s spaghetti. Ginger ate two platefuls. It sounded like she and Mom would be coming the next few Saturdays for swimming lessons, dinner, and stenciling.

When it was time to go, Grant reminded them, "Don't forget, brunch after church tomorrow."

Her mother laughed. "I'm not apt to forget."

Uh-oh, Ginger thought, remembering that they'd even invited Gram to the restaurant. What was coming now? Ginger had a sinking feeling that she knew what it was.

The next morning Grant stopped by to pick them up for church. Joshua, Lilabet, and Grandfather Gabriel waited in the car. "Hi," Ginger said, a little more at ease with them now. They greeted her brightly, as if they liked her better, too.

Grant said, "I talked to Katie this morning. She's going to watch for you at Sunday school."

Ginger bristled. How'd he know she'd be willing to go? He'd interfered and ruined her good feelings. She almost said so, but Mom gave her a don't-you-dare look.

"How nice you look in a dress," Grandfather Gabriel said as Ginger sat down beside him in the backseat.

"I guess it's not too bad for a dress," she said. It

79

was white with tiny green and pink squiggles. Gram had made it for today's brunch, which made Ginger all the more suspicious.

When they arrived at church, Ginger found her own way to the classroom she'd been in for the Good News Club. At the door, Katie hurried over to her. "Hey, I saved you a seat!"

She turned to the teacher whose blonde hair curled up at her shoulders.

"This is Mrs. Tyler."

"Hi," Ginger said. "How come Miss Birmingham isn't here?"

Mrs. Tyler smiled. "She just teaches on Wednesday evenings."

"Oh," Ginger replied. She remembered Mom saying these teachers were volunteers, which meant they didn't even get paid for their work.

The class started and they sang, "This is the day that the Lord has made. . . ." Ginger struggled to follow along in the songbook.

"God loves you," Mrs. Tyler said, "and He has a wonderful plan for your life." She said it as though she really believed it. "Let's look up John 3:16 in our Bibles."

Katie found the place easily and shared her Bible with Ginger. "God so loved the world that He gave His only begotten son, that whoever believes in Him should not perish, but have eternal life."

"That shows how much God loves each of us," Mrs. Tyler explained. "God loves you so much He sent Jesus here to earth. When you believe Him to be your rescuer and everyday friend, your life can turn into a wonderful adventure."

Ginger's mind wandered to Mom and Grant and Grandfather Gabriel. They'd be sitting in church together, the three of them, listening to the minister. She wondered why this church's minister wore a suit instead of a robe. Then she thought about what a nice day she was missing at the beach.

After a while Mrs. Tyler said, "Time for crafts."

To Ginger's surprise, they stenciled. But instead of hearts and flowers, it was pictures of green pine trees and a brown tent. On top, they stenciled in green: "SUMMER CAMP."

One thing that's sure, she thought, *I'm not going to camp!* As soon as she had a chance, she folded up her picture and, when no one was watching, she jammed it into the wastebasket.

Considering everything, Sunday school hadn't been too bad, Ginger decided later as she got into Grant's car. She felt guilty when she saw that Lilabet had drawn a scribbly picture in her class. Then Joshua showed his father a picture exactly like the one she'd stenciled about summer camp.

"Didn't you do any artwork, Ginger?" her mother asked.

"I forgot it," Ginger lied, then felt terrible.

Grandfather Gabriel asked Joshua, "Are you going to summer camp again this year?"

"If I can," Joshua said. "The other guys are."

"Is Katie going?" Ginger's mother asked.

"I don't know," Ginger replied. At least that was true.

They drove out of the church parking lot and down toward Ocean Avenue. For a while they rode alongside the ocean, then Grant said, "Here we are . . . the Sandpiper Hotel."

They pulled into the drive of the elegant ocean-side hotel. At the entrance, a uniformed doorman helped them from the car.

Gram awaited them in the lobby, looking nice in a new lavender dress. "I was afraid I had the wrong time," she said.

"Not at all, we're a little late," Mom answered. She introduced Gram to everyone.

"Did you come by taxi, Mrs. Trumbell?" Grandfather inquired.

"No, I'm a walker," Gram said. "Ginger and I walk a lot along the ocean, don't we?"

Ginger nodded. Her stomach was rumbling, and she was glad to see they were headed straight for the dining room.

A hostess checked off Grant's name. "This way, please." She led them to a lovely dining room and seated them at a window table with an ocean view. Someone brought a booster chair for Lilabet, and a busboy filled their goblets with ice water. The hostess said, "Please help yourselves to the buffet."

Joshua glanced mischievously at Ginger, and he

murmured, "Don't mind if we do."

She smiled. "I guess you're hungry, too."

Grandfather Gabriel grinned at them. "Me, too."

At the buffet, Ginger helped herself to strawberries, a chocolate muffin, and sweet rolls. She passed by the silver dishes of salads, scrambled eggs, bacon, and sausages, but she did take some lasagna, meatballs, and chicken. She was glad to see Joshua had piled his plate even higher than hers.

Finally everyone was seated at the table again. Grandfather Gabriel, sitting across from her, said grace. He ended with, "We thank You, Father, for this beautiful day and this special occasion. In Christ's name we pray. Amen."

Ginger noticed another lovesick look pass between her mother and Grant, but she tried to forget about it as she ate.

Beside her Gram asked, "Isn't this lovely?"

"I guess it is," Ginger answered.

Before long, she and Joshua returned to the buffet. She took cherry pie, cheesecake, two brownies, three pieces of white fudge, and a small cluster of grapes to look nutritious.

After finishing all of it, she couldn't eat another thing. She sat back while the busboy poured more ice water into her goblet. Across the table Grandfather Gabriel winked at her, and she grinned.

After a moment he stood up, and everyone quieted. In his deep voice he said, "It gives me great pleasure to tell all of you some wonderful news. As

83

you might suspect, we have two people with us who are very much in love. I am privileged to announce the engagement of Sallie Virginia Trumbell to my son, Grant Matthew Gabriel. And, now, if we might drink a toast—"

Ginger's heart plummeted. The very worst was coming true.

Lilabet said, "What a pretty ring!"

Ginger stared at the ring sparkling on her mother's hand. When had she gotten it?

Gram said, "I'm so happy for you, Sallie!"

How could she? Ginger thought. How could Gram be happy when *Dad* was her own son . . . when Dad was Mom's *real* husband?

Grant rose to his feet. "I'd like to propose a toast to Sallie, to this wonderful woman I've come to love . . . whom my whole family has come to love."

Tears welled in Ginger's eyes, and she blinked hard to stop them. Maybe next Mom would have to stand and say that the two of them loved Grant— and it wasn't true!

Grant looked at Ginger. "And to Miss Ginger Anne Trumbell, whom I've come to love, too."

Ginger felt a weird smile forming, then she bit down on her lower lip. Maybe she'd begun to like them just a little, but she didn't *love* the Gabriels . . . not a one of them. If Grant thought he was going to marry Mom, he could just take back his ring . . . and this brunch and everything. If there was any marrying at all, Mom would marry Dad again!

8

The next Saturday Dad was out of town again, and Ginger felt more and more upset. Mom wouldn't listen to her at all about not getting married. Not one bit.

On Sunday after church Grant wanted to stop at Santa Rosita Christian, so Ginger went in with Mom and him. In the office, Mom glanced at the school's new fall brochure. "What a fine job you've done on this," she said.

Ginger felt uneasy as she read "Catch Our SPIRIT!" on the white folder. An embossed white bird soared over the words "Santa Rosita Christian School."

Her mother glanced through the papers in the

folder. "I'm certainly impressed with these test scores," she remarked. "I knew the kids did well, but I didn't realize they ranked this much higher than the national averages."

"We're proud of them," Grant replied. "Take a look at our new computer lab program." After they'd discussed that, he said, "Think I'll take this page about the fifth- and sixth-grade athletic program home for Josh."

Fifth- and sixth-grades? Ginger wondered.

Joshua was in sixth grade, but why would Grant mention fifth grade unless he was talking about her? She snapped, "I'm not going to school here!"

"Why, you're not even enrolled here, Ginger," her mother said. "You're signed up to return to Santa Rosita Elementary."

"Good," Ginger said and drew a relieved breath.

As the week continued, her mother planned and shopped every day; she chose wedding invitations, announcements, clothes, and everything else. Instead of asking Ginger to approve of the marriage, she'd say, "Should I wear a cream-colored dress for the wedding?" and "You'll look perfect in a peach junior bridesmaid dress."

"A junior bridesmaid dress!" Ginger repeated. It was the first she'd even heard about it.

"There's no one in the world I'd rather have for my bridesmaid," Mom said. "Please don't let me down. Please."

She sounded so hopeful it melted Ginger's heart a

little, but not entirely. "You know I hate pink," she said.

"But peach isn't pink," her mother explained. "There's an enormous difference. I can't imagine you in some shades of pink, either."

Mom was waiting for an answer, so Ginger finally said, "I don't care!"

Her mother dropped a kiss on her forehead. "You'll look wonderful in peach with your beautiful red hair."

"I'll look terrible!" Ginger snapped. If she didn't feel so guilty about causing Mom's and Dad's divorce, she'd say a lot more than that! Instead, maybe she'd cut her hair off to the scalp. Wouldn't that fix everyone! Anyhow, Dad would be home on Saturday, and that'd be the end of the wedding plans. He'd be so jealous, he'd want to remarry Mom real fast.

But the next Saturday, Dad was out of town again.

Grant and Mom mowed Gram's lawn. In the afternoon, Grant gave Ginger and Katie another swimming lesson while Mom stenciled in Lilabet's room. It seemed to Ginger that they were always with the Gabriels.

On the Fourth of July, Grandfather Gabriel went to a ball game with friends. Grant took the rest of them, even Gram, to the county fair. Excited, Ginger hadn't thought about her father all morning, but when Grant parked his car in the fairground lot, she wished it were Dad taking them. When she was little, he always took them to the fair.

Once they stepped through the turnstiles, though, she forgot about Dad. Overhead, bright red and blue and yellow and green sky cars glided by against the sky. In front of them, a Dixieland band played and a strawhatted man sang, "Look away, look away, look away, Dixieland!" Everywhere booths echoed with "Hot dogs!" "Popcorn!" and "Get your cotton candy here!" From the Fun Zone, carnival music and whirling rides added to the hubbub.

"*Balloons!*" Lilabet yelled. She pointed at a clown selling colorful helium balloons.

Grant teased, "Would you like to have a balloon, Lilabet!"

Lilabet's brown eyes widened. "Please can I, Daddy?"

Grant laughed. "You certainly may. I'm glad you still have inexpensive tastes."

Cotton candy! Ginger wanted to yell out herself, seeing fair goers eating it as they strolled through the crowd.

While Grant bought a silver and red balloon for Lilabet, Gram reached for Ginger's hand. She gave her some folding money and closed her fingers around it. "Take it so you can buy yourself whatever you want, Ginger. Spend it like you're rich!"

"Thanks, Gram!" Ginger smiled appreciatively and slipped the bills into her pocket.

Grant said, "Gram, Sallie and I thought we'd go to the flower show first. And Lilabet would probably enjoy seeing real cows and chickens so she knows they're not just pictures in books. What else shall we see?"

Gram hesitated. "The rest of you don't have to go with me, but I'd love to see the clothing and food exhibits!"

"We'll have time for everything," Mom answered as she tied the balloon to Lilabet's wrist. "I'd like to see the photography and art displays myself."

Ginger's spirits sank. Exhibits and farm animals were okay, but not very exciting. Besides, she'd seen them before.

Grant turned to her and Joshua. "How'd the two of you like to go on the Fun Zone rides?"

Joshua's brown eyes sparkled. "Sure!"

"Can we really?" Ginger asked.

"Of course you may," her mother assured her.

Grant gave some money to Joshua. "It's for both of you," he said. "Be careful of pickpockets."

Joshua put the bills into his wallet, and stuck it in his front jeans pocket to be safe.

"Thanks a lot!" Ginger said to Grant.

"My pleasure," he said.

Last year she'd only gone on tame rides with Mom and Mandy. This would be lots better, with no grown-ups to hold them back. Best of all, Joshua didn't seem to mind going with her.

Grant said, "We'll meet right here by the

Dixieland Bandstand at five o'clock."

"All right!" Ginger and Joshua replied almost at once.

"Have fun!" Mom and Gram called after them.

This time, they answered together, "We will!"

On the way to the Fun Zone, Ginger realized she hadn't had much time alone with Joshua except when they played ping-pong. Maybe he'd say something again about them helping each other out. Maybe he didn't want Mom and Grant to get married, either. But now was no time for that kind of talk. Anyhow, she'd let Joshua bring it up. He was older, and she guessed he was smart, since Mom said he made mostly A's at school.

"Let's start on the Ferris wheel," Joshua said over the loud carnival music swirling from the midway. "It's tame, but when we're up on top, we can look around and see what else we'd like to ride."

"Sounds like a good idea," she answered.

While he stood in line to buy the ride tickets, Ginger bought pink cotton candy for each of them. Carnival music filled the air, and rides roared and whirled. *There's nothing as much fun as a fair*, she thought. Besides, it helped her not to think about other things.

It seemed only moments before they were settled into their seat on the Ferris wheel and heading upward. Then they were on the top, stopping with a jerk, swinging over the whole fairgrounds.

"Wow!" Ginger exclaimed.

"Look over by the grandstand," Joshua said. "They're having horse races on the track. And look over there by the animal barns. It's a tractor pull contest."

"I always like to see how little the horses and tractors and people look from here," Ginger replied. She bit into her cotton candy. It was just right, cottony and sweet.

"How about a fast ride next?" Joshua asked. "Or do you get sick on that kind?"

"Not me!" Ginger returned. "I'm not afraid of any ride anywhere! How about you?"

"Not me either!" Joshua laughed. "I was afraid maybe you wouldn't like the wild rides. I should have known better. Let's not waste time on any more of these tame ones."

The Ferris wheel started again, and they circled down through the racket of the excited crowds and up again. "All right!" she yelled. It was wonderful to see the entire fairgrounds, Santa Rosita's golden hillsides, and the great Pacific Ocean in the distance.

The Ferris wheel started down, and Ginger's eyes turned to the rides below. Nearby, the Twister looked like the wildest; it twisted and whipped the riders upside down. "Listen to those kids scream," she said. "Let's try the Twister first!"

On the Twister, the Fun Zone turned into an upside-down world. When it stopped, Ginger's head was still spinning crazily.

91

"Let's do it again!" she yelled.

When they finally took a rest from the rides, they tried the midway games. At one booth, they pitched balls at moving tenpins, and Ginger won a stuffed brown lion. "Fair Lion," she said. "I'm going to name him Fair Lion."

With the next pitch, Joshua won a lion himself.

By five o'clock Ginger had had her fill of being bounced and whipped about. She and Joshua arrived at the Dixieland Bandstand just as Grant, Mom, Gram, and Lilabet were settling on the chairs to hear the music.

"Here they are," Grant said. "Right on time, too. We thought we'd go over to the Mexican Village for dinner. We can sit out on the grass there to eat, then go over to the grandstand for the evening show."

Two hours later, they sat in the grandstand where twangy country music filled the air. With the sun setting over the ocean in the distance and Fair Lion on her lap, Ginger thought this was the best Fourth of July she'd ever had.

At last, darkness fell all around them, and the announcer said, "Let the fireworks begin! Happy Fourth of July!"

The band played patriotic music, and great bursts of silver and gold flared against the dark sky, followed by bright sprays of reds and greens. Burst after burst of brilliant colors filled the sky. Lilabet sat on Grant's lap, clapping. "Ooooo!" she called out with the rest of the crowd.

Ginger and Joshua joined in, ooooooing as the colors crackled and sparkled in the night sky, then laughing so people knew they were only acting crazy.

Ginger hoped the fireworks would never end. On and on they went, gloriously bursting against the darkness. At last, for the finale, a great red, white, and blue flag sparkled against the darkness while the crowd sang "The Star-Spangled Banner."

Not caring what people thought, Ginger sang out with all of her might: "Oh, say does that star-spangled banner yet wave . . . o'er the land of the free . . . and the home . . . of the brave!"

Firecrackers crackled, and fireworks flared as they boomed across the sky in bursts of red, white, and blue.

Finally it was over, and everyone cheered.

When the grandstand lights came on, Ginger's spirits still soared. "Wasn't that something?!" people asked. "Wasn't it glorious?!"

At length, the crowd quieted and streamed out of the grandstand. Ginger began to feel calmer as they walked through the dimly lit parking lot. Slowly and silently, the truth came to her: it had been a wonderful day, but nothing had changed. Mom and Grant were still getting married, and Joshua hadn't said a word about it.

She gazed at the shadowy scene before them. Grant carried a tired Lilabet on his shoulders, her balloon bobbing in the darkness; Mom and Gram walked along on either side of them. It was quieter now, even though lines of cars edged out toward the exit. She would have to talk to Joshua now. She swallowed hard. "Joshua . . ."

He turned to her, and she made herself go on, not quite seeing the expression on his face. "Remember the Sunday that Mom and I met you at your grandfather's old church?"

"Sure," he answered.

She rushed on. "You said maybe we could help each other. I thought you meant to stop my mom and your dad—" Even in the shadowy light she could see he was frowning. She snapped, "Well, *you* said it, not me!"

"I changed my mind," he said. "I decided that I . . . that I like your mother a lot."

"But if they get married, everything will be different!" she replied in shock.

"It'll be all right."

"But it won't—it won't! Everything will be ruined!"

Joshua answered, "I don't think it will."

I know it will! I know it! she thought. Everything around her turned black with hopelessness. Her family and the crowd around them moved on, but she felt frozen in place.

"Hey, Ginger, come on!" Joshua shouted back to her.

The rest of them halted and turned toward her.

"Ginger, stay with us!" her mother called out.

94

"You'll get lost back there."

"You all right, Ginger?" Grant asked.

She started forward again, stumbling on a rut but catching her balance. "Yeah," she answered. "Yeah, I'm all right."

But she wasn't all right. She'd lied again, and everything felt like darkness. Only this darkness was ten times darker after the exciting day and the glorious fireworks. She'd never ever in all her life felt so hopeless.

9

"Ginger, what's wrong with you lately?" Mom asked at dinner one evening. "You've been moping ever since the fair."

Ginger pushed her peas around the plate with her fork. *Can't you guess what's wrong?* she thought.

"You've never lost interest in eating before," Mom said. "I hurried home from work to cook your favorite chicken casserole, and now you won't even eat it."

"I'm sorry," Ginger said. "I'm not hungry."

She remembered the time before the divorce when Mom had cried every night in her bedroom. Gram had said, "If you don't pull out of this, Sallie, you're going to have a nervous breakdown!"

Whatever a nervous breakdown was, it sounded a lot worse than just crying.

Now Mom said, "Ginger, we have to discuss Grant and me. I've tried and tried—"

"No!" Ginger cried, rising up from the kitchen counter. "I don't want to talk about it!" It'd be better to be miserable herself than to make Mom that unhappy again.

"Don't you like Grant and the children?" Mom asked.

"They're okay."

"Then why are you so upset?" Mom asked.

Ginger made herself sit down again. "I don't want to talk about it. Anyhow, I'm beginning to feel hungry."

She made herself eat.

Dad was the only answer to the problem, she told herself again. Before, when she'd talked to him about Mom and Grant, he didn't know how serious things were. He had to come soon!

The next Saturday, however, he wasn't in town again. Nor the next. *Dad, when are you coming?* Ginger's heart cried out. *When, when, when, when?*

His absence didn't seem to bother Gram. During the week, her sewing machine hummed endlessly. "I haven't had such a good time sewing in ages," she declared as she sewed.

A good time? Ginger didn't see how working day and night could be a good time. Besides her usual sewing work, Gram was turning out more and more clothes for the wedding: Mom's wedding dress, Ginger's, and a matching peach-colored flower girl dress for Lilabet, not to mention Mom's traveling clothes. Every day it was, "Ginger, we have to shop for thread," or "Let's go out for sewing machine needles." Then it was, "I'm so busy, could you make us a salad?" and "How about running out for hamburgers?"

Next came ordering flowers for the wedding, then shopping for shoes to dye peach like Ginger's junior bridesmaid dress. Peach, she decided unhappily, was an awful lot like pink, no matter what Mom said.

At night when Mom arrived home from work, the phone rang and rang. Nana and Grandpa Allan might come from Virginia, and maybe Aunt Rosie. Anyhow, Ginger didn't see why they were so excited when Dad would surely stop the wedding.

The only calm times, it seemed, were at Good News Club, Sunday school, and on Saturday afternoons when Grant gave her and Katie swimming lessons. During those calm times, everything felt a little better. Even Katie was beginning to seem like a friend.

"I surely am glad we're having swimming lessons together, Ginger," Katie said one Saturday in the pool.

Ginger said, "I am, too."

Katie smiled. "The very best thing for me this

summer has been meeting you."

"Yeah?" Ginger asked. "I guess I didn't think it might be a strange summer for you, too. Did you want to leave Georgia?"

"I surely *didn't* want to leave," Katie answered, as if she hadn't had much choice.

"I know all about that," Ginger answered unhappily. She didn't have much choice about Mom getting married, either.

"I do believe I'm finally getting used to living here. Anyhow, we're supposed to count our blessings, and you're one of mine." Katie smiled and splashed water at Ginger.

Ginger splashed water back. Katie was all right.

Then even Saturday afternoons were ruined. Mom and Grant decided to have a wedding party—a reception, they called it. It would be at the Gabriel house. Suddenly painters were working everywhere. Before and after swimming lessons, Ginger tried to ignore all of it as she dodged them and their paint buckets and ladders. Then Grandfather Gabriel decided to move into the guest house behind the pool, and workmen began to hammer there.

By the beginning of August, she and Katie could swim across the pool. Mom had finished stenciling in Lilabet's room and was busy finding new furnishings for the house. Not that she planned to change a lot—she liked the dark antiques Grant had inherited from his mother's family. She especially liked his mother's collection of angels—carved wooden ones, others made of crystal, straw and metal, even paintings of angels. It seemed Mom liked everything about the Gabriels. She asked Ginger, "You sure you don't want a canopied bed for your room?"

"I *hate* canopied beds!" Ginger snapped.

"Ginger, you're just being difficult," her mother said. "You know we'd like to give you a beautiful bedroom, within reason, of course. You can choose the colors now."

"I like my brown bedroom just fine!"

Her mother kissed the top of her head. "Ginger, I do love you. I know this must be difficult for you. After the wedding, things will be more normal."

Ginger's heart cried out, *Dad, please come home! Please come and stop everything now!*

The next Friday morning Gram said, "Your dad phoned last night. He's being transferred to Hawaii. I'm supposed to tell you he's sorry he can't see you. He's awfully busy."

"He's moving to Hawaii?" Ginger cried.

Gram nodded. "He'll certainly see you before he goes. And Ginger—"

Ginger looked up at Gram.

"He might get married, too. He's thinking about marrying someone else."

"*Someone else!*" Ginger felt like a soccer ball had slammed into her chest.

Gram nodded. "It sounds that way, but he may just be reacting to your mother's wedding."

Ginger cried out, *"What about me, Gram? What about me? He was supposed to come home and stop the wedding!"*

"Ginger, I know how difficult—"

Ginger didn't want to hear another word about how difficult things were. Her mother was marrying Grant Gabriel, and Dad might marry someone else! Everything was terrible, terrible! "I hate him . . . I hate him!" she yelled.

"Ginger, get hold of yourself," Gram told her. "Your mother's wedding is just over a week away."

"A week away!" For the first time, the truth of it hit her. "No!" she cried out. "No!"

She ran blindly out of the house, the back door banging behind her. She ran down Gram's block, then the next, and barely crossed Ocean Avenue on the green light. She ran toward the beach, not knowing what to do. As she raced along, she realized that Mom and Dad wouldn't change, and Gram wouldn't help either. Nothing could stop the wedding.

Suddenly an idea hit. *God.* Everyone thought He could do anything. Maybe He would do a miracle. Still running, she prayed, *God, if You're really there, stop Mom's wedding! Stop it now, please!*

Guilt stabbed her, and she truly felt sorry for every bad thing she'd ever done. *I'm sorry about my bad temper and lying . . . and not always minding*

101

Mom. . . . Not caring that people stared at her, she ran on and on, down the steep path to the beach, her feet tangling in the ice plant. Trying to remember what she'd learned in Sunday school, she prayed with all of her heart, *Jesus, rescue me!*

At the bottom of the path, her heart pounded so hard she had to sit down on the hot sand. She sat and panted, knees to her chest, until her breath came more steadily.

After a while, she became aware of the warm salty air and the ocean's deep thundering. The sun shone brilliantly, and the blue water glistened as far out as she could see.

God understands, Ginger realized with a sudden flash. *He understands about me.* To her amazement, her heart no longer ached so with anguish; instead it began to feel clean. It felt as if she were being forgiven.

Before long, her spirit grew stronger and stronger. She stood up and slowly walked in the warm sunshine toward the surf. To her astonishment, she saw everything around her with new eyes. The sky and the sea were more beautiful than she'd ever realized . . . even the sand under her feet seemed polished with beauty. And how good the soft breeze felt as it brushed against her arms and legs. She'd never seen things so clearly, nor felt such wonder over the breeze and the sunshine. Even ordinary old gulls that cawed and swooped over the trash cans were transformed into a wondrous sight.

Ginger began to stroll alongside the surf. Great waves thundered in from afar and broke as they neared land; slowing, they turned into gentle swells that lapped onto the sand and left bubbles bright with rainbows. *God planned it like that*, Ginger thought. He'd made the ocean and the beaches and even the bubbly rainbows. In Sunday school, they said He cared about her and everyone else, too. He loved her, Ginger Anne Trumbell. *Thank You, God*, she thought. *Thank You!*

A man called out from the distance, his voice familiar.

Still full of wonder, it took Ginger a moment to realize he was calling her. Turning, she saw Grandfather Gabriel jogging toward her on the beach. How strange that he'd come now.

Nearing her, he slowed down to a walk. "I thought it might be you, Virginia. I'm so pleased to see you."

"I didn't know you came here," Ginger said.

He puffed a little. "I usually jog along the street at home, but this morning I felt an urge to be out along the ocean." He smiled. "Time for me to slow down now. Want to walk with me?"

She beamed. "Sure."

He eyed her curiously, then remarked, "You look happier than you have lately."

She could feel her eyes dancing. "I sure am."

He guessed, "You've met the Lord!"

She smiled and nodded. "I asked Jesus to rescue

me, like I learned in Sunday school."

"Then you have!" he exclaimed. "That's just what we've been praying for!"

She wanted to tell him all about it, but she didn't know where to begin. She could only say, "I feel . . . wonderful."

"That's from God's forgiveness when you receive Jesus," Grandfather Gabriel said. "He loves all of us so much that He forgives us and even changes our hearts."

"Mine feels like sunshine and rainbows now," she told him. "I guess it's . . . gladness."

"It's joy," he said, "pure joy. Christians should be the most joyous people on earth. And they are if they give their whole hearts to Jesus."

"I am . . . oh, I am now!" Joy bubbled over in her heart, bubbling brighter than the foamy rainbows on the beach.

Grandfather Gabriel looked joyous himself. "A great woman, Lady Julia of Norwich, once said, 'The fullness of joy is to behold God in everything.' It means seeing God's hand everywhere, in everything."

Looking around her, Ginger knew what he meant. She'd already seen God's hand in making the sea, the sky, the sand, and even the sea gulls.

"I believe God arranged for me to come to the beach this morning to be with you," Grandfather Gabriel said.

Somehow she knew it was true. "I think so, too."

"What a special time this is for me," he told her. "I'll always remember He brought us here together now."

"Me too," she said.

"I hope you'll always see God in everything," Grandfather said. "Not everyone who calls himself a Christian does, but I pray you'll be one of those who do. And I pray you'll see life . . . and others through God's love, too."

"I hope so," Ginger responded. "Oh, I hope so!"

"If you stay close to the Lord, you're in for an adventurous life," Grandfather said.

Ginger couldn't imagine what adventure might happen to her next. What could be half as exciting as getting to know God?

10

Ginger gazed at the orange, gold, and pink sunset through the Sandpiper Hotel's dining room window. Beside her, Joshua seemed to realize she was no longer fighting the wedding, but he knew enough not to mention it. On the other side of her, Mom and Grant beamed at each other. Mom's parents, Nana and Grandpa Allan, sat across from them; they'd just arrived from Virginia with Mom's younger sister, Aunt Rosie. Everyone at the table buzzed with excitement.

Grandfather Gabriel, seated across from Ginger, asked, "How's everything, Virginia?"

"Fine, I guess, thanks."

It was nice to let God change her on the inside, but sometimes she still lost her temper. If only God would change her outside so she'd no longer be all knees, legs, and elbows like she'd been an hour ago at the wedding rehearsal. She sure didn't want to be like that tomorrow at the wedding.

Nana Allan's reddish-brown hair shone in the sunlight. "I didn't know anyone called you Virginia," she said, pleased. "It's my middle name and your mother's."

"Grandfather Gabriel's the only one who calls me that," Ginger replied. "I mean . . . well, other people could, too, if they want."

Grandpa Allan, who was plump and jolly, said, "I'm tempted to be a little jealous, but I'm glad you'll have one grandfather nearby. He looks like a trustworthy fellow."

Ginger laughed. "I guess he is."

Grandfather Gabriel grinned at her from across the table. They'd talked for a long time that day on the beach. One thing he'd told her was that most kids felt it was their fault if their parents got a divorce—but it almost never was.

Another thing he'd said was, "Just because you're a Christian now, don't think you'll be perfect. Remember only Christ was. There'll still be a lot of the old Ginger in you."

Old Ginger was right! But she loved people more now. Sometimes even the ugliest people looked beautiful when she remembered that God loved them, too. Best of all, she'd forgiven her father for not being there when she really needed him.

Grandfather Gabriel spoke. "Looks like we'll all survive the wedding."

"I hope so," Ginger replied. "I've never even seen one, and now I'm going to be the junior bridesmaid!"

"Weddings are nice," Grandpa Allan observed, "but usually everyone's glad when they're over."

I sure will be, Ginger thought.

Mom said, "I'm afraid poor Ginger has put up with a lot, but she's holding up better than I dreamed."

Ginger hid a smile. She hadn't told anyone except Grandfather that she was a Christian. It seemed better to wait until the bustle of the wedding was over. Besides, he'd said she could tell the others when the time was right.

Her mother said, "This week has been wild, hasn't it?"

"It sure has," Ginger replied. "Everything's flying by." Gram had finished all of the dresses, but there'd been a mix-up about Ginger's shoe color, so they had to buy white ones. Then the florist wanted to change flowers. This morning they'd rushed to the airport to pick up Nana, Grandpa Allan, and Aunt Rosie. The phone rang and rang. If Mom hadn't take off an extra week, they'd never have made it.

A waiter served everyone at the table, and Grant said, "Dad, would you say grace?"

Grandfather Gabriel bowed his head. "Heavenly

108

Father," he began in his nice deep voice. "We come to You with praise and thanksgiving this special evening before Sallie's and Grant's wedding. We thank You for this bountiful food, and we thank You for Your love, which we see reflected between them. We ask that tomorrow You will give us grace and wisdom as we play our roles in the wedding. We thank You in the name of Your beloved Son and our Lord and Savior, Jesus Christ. Amen."

Ginger wasn't sure if "grace" meant "graceful," but that's what she hoped to be tomorrow: as graceful as a junior bridesmaid should be. If she had a wad of gum in her mouth right now, she'd agree by giving it a loud crack.

Saturday morning zigzagged by like lightning. At one-thirty, Ginger gazed at herself in the full-length mirror. Was the girl in the peach junior bridesmaid dress really her? Nana Allan had brushed her hair so it didn't look too wild, then placed the halo of real flowers on her head. Her white shoes and white lace stockings looked perfect with the white and peach-colored flowers in her bouquet and halo. And Mom let her wear pale peach lipstick and nail polish.

Aunt Rosie hadn't known if she could come until last week, so she wasn't in the wedding. It was a shame, since she was as pretty as Mom, though her hair was redder. Aunt Rosie said, "Ginger Trumbell, you look perfect."

Ginger grinned at her reflection in the mirror.

She didn't look too bad. Not even all legs, knees, and elbows.

Mom stepped to the mirror beside her. She wore her cream-colored silk wedding dress and the halo of peach and white flowers in her hair.

"Oh, Mom, you really look beautiful," Ginger said.

"Thank you . . . so do you. But what's more important, you don't seem quite so set against my marrying Grant. I've prayed and prayed for God to change your heart about it. You don't mind the marriage so much now, do you?"

Ginger's eyes clouded, and she shook her head. She wanted to say God had changed her heart about it, but Aunt Rosie was right there beside them. Instead she asked, "Mom, this time you're getting married, is it for always?"

"Yes, Ginger," Mom said, "for always, forever and ever."

Almost like what Grandfather had said to her about Jesus: "He'll never leave you, nor forsake you."

At last they were ready. Grandpa Allan announced, "Time to leave for the church, ladies!"

At the curb, Aunt Rosie helped Nana into Mom's car. Behind them, Grandpa Allan helped Ginger and her mother into the backseat of his car. "Ah, the life of a chauffeur!" he joked.

Mom sang out gaily, "Get me to the church on time!"

"You can count on that," Grandpa Allan said, then turned serious. "Do we have the bouquets?"

"Rosie has them in my car," Mom assured him.

Had it been like this when Mom married Dad, Ginger wondered. And was he thinking about them now? Was he thinking about Mom getting married? Of course, they hadn't been married in a church—*Stop thinking about that!* she told herself. Grandfather Gabriel had said, "Learn from the past, and then put it behind you." That's what she wanted to do.

"We're off!" Grandpa Allan announced.

The familiar blocks disappeared in a blur, and before long they drove up behind Santa Rosita Community Church. They climbed carefully out of the car and hurried for the back door.

Inside, organ music already filled the sanctuary.

Her mother said, "We wait here, in this back room."

A minute later, Katie's mother brought in Lilabet. "How beautiful y'all look!" she said in her soft southern voice. "I better run now! I'll be praying for y'all!"

"Oh, Lilabet, aren't you a pretty flower girl!" Mom said.

Lilabet wore a fluffy peach dress with lots of ribbons and bows. She peered up at them and nodded. "I look pretty, but not like a flower!"

Ginger almost laughed out loud.

Before long, an usher arrived to escort Nana up

the aisle to her seat. She threw kisses to Mom and Ginger as she left.

Mom asked, "Ready, Ginger and Lilabet?"

Ginger nodded. If Lilabet made a mistake, she'd have to help. You never knew what Lilabet might do. Last night when they'd practiced, she'd run wildly down the church aisle. *Please, God, don't let Lilabet act crazy*, Ginger prayed.

The opening chords of the "Bridal March" resounded through the sanctuary, and Mom said, "Time for you to go, Lilabet. Don't forget to throw the rose petals from your basket."

Lilabet smiled brightly and started down the aisle.

Ginger held the door open a crack to peek out. Grandfather Gabriel stood before the altar with Grant and Joshua, all three of them handsome in dark suits. They watched Lilabet's progress up the aisle. Ginger guessed they were praying for Lilabet not to act crazy, too.

Lilabet hurried up the aisle, beginning to run. The guests laughed, and she stopped. Looking at them, she slowly started forward again, remembering to scatter the rose petals. When she'd finished, she ran into Grant's arms. "All done!" she piped.

The guests burst out laughing.

Grant kissed her and carried her to sit with Aunt Rosie.

Grandpa Allan said, "You're next, Ginger."

Ginger swallowed hard and started down the

aisle, remembering to smile. She paused in time with the music, but her bouquet shook. *Please, God,* she prayed, *don't let them laugh at me, too.* She'd no more than prayed the words than she knew she'd been thinking about herself again. It was more important to please God, and to please Mom and Grant.

The guests murmured appreciatively as she passed, but she kept her eyes on Grandfather Gabriel, Grant, and Joshua. They beamed at her. This was her new family, and God loved all of them—and suddenly so did she! She felt she might burst with joy. Stopping in place, she turned and beamed at the guests.

Seven triumphal notes sounded, and everyone turned to watch Grandpa Allan escort Mom down the aisle. She looked like an angel in her cream-colored silk dress and flowered halo. As she moved toward them, her eyes touched upon all of them with love, then turned to Grant. Their gaze held so much love that instead of thinking *Yuck*, Ginger had to blink hard.

Grandfather Gabriel began the service. "Dearly beloved, we are gathered here in the sight of God and man. . . ."

The wonderful words flowed all around them, binding them together into a new family. Then Mom and Grant exchanged rings, and Grandfather Gabriel said, "Those whom God hath joined together, let not man put asunder."

Ginger knew in her heart that this time everything would be right. *Thank You, God, for changing my heart. Thank You, thank You!*

The reception at the Gabriel house wasn't formal, but everything looked nice, Ginger thought as she stepped in the front door. In the living room, she stopped. More wedding gifts! Guests had piled beautifully wrapped wedding presents near the fireplace.

Suddenly it occurred to her—she hadn't bought anything for Mom and Grant . . . not one single thing! Lots of gifts had come in the past two weeks and were open and on display in the far end of the living room, but somehow they hadn't made her think of buying a gift herself. Heartsick, Ginger started for the dining room.

Aunt Rosie served pink fruit punch from the big glass punch bowl at the far side of the table. "You look so lovely, Ginger," she said. She handed her a cup of punch. "Wasn't it a beautiful wedding?"

"Yeah," Ginger agreed, gulping the punch.

Aunt Rosie added, "Help yourself to the canapés."

"Canapés?"

"They're tiny gourmet sandwiches," Aunt Rosie explained. She nodded toward the other side of the table where platters of the dainty delicacies stood. "There's cress, cucumber—"

"I guess I don't feel hungry now," Ginger said. What could she do about a wedding present?

114

"Hey, Ginger!" Katie called out, then she laughed. "I thought I'd find you by the food." They hadn't seen each other since their swimming lessons had ended two weeks ago. "Your mother told me there are tiny pizzas out in the family room."

"That sounds better than cress or cucumber canapés!"

Katie said, "You look so dressed up, I thought maybe you wouldn't want just plain old pizza."

"Not me," Ginger answered, though she still didn't feel hungry. As they started for the family room, she was tempted to tell Katie that she hadn't bought a wedding present, but she decided not to share her trouble.

Katie said, "You really look nice in peach."

"Thanks. I decided I like it after all."

Katie's brown eyes widened. "You do?"

"I think I want pale peach to be the color of my bedroom. Maybe I'll have a canopied bed, but I don't know yet."

"Hey, you're teasing!" Katie exclaimed. "I thought you hated pink."

"Peach is different. Besides, my mind's been changing about lots of things lately." She even felt different about living here now. Sure, she'd miss her old house, but she could always visit Gram near the beach.

Lilabet ran into the family room from outside. "Piz-za!" she sang out. "Piz-za . . . piz-za . . . I love piz-za!" She grabbed a slice from the table.

115

Joshua had followed her in, and he rolled his eyes skyward again. "Dad said I have to keep track of her."

"We will for a while," Ginger offered, then turned to Katie. "All right with you?"

"It surely is," Katie replied, nibbling on a pizza.

Joshua looked surprised. "Thanks. How about a game of ping-pong later, Ginger? I've been practicing."

"Okay." She couldn't play as hard wearing her junior bridesmaid dress, but she guessed she could still beat him. She selected a small pizza and hoped she could eat it.

After a while everyone gathered around the dining room to watch Mom and Grant cut the three-layered wedding cake.

"Speech, speech!" the guests called out.

"Unaccustomed as I am to speaking," Grant began, and everyone laughed. When they quieted, he grew serious. "I don't know if ever a man was so blessed, to have two such special families joined together. Maybe our lives won't always be as perfect as today has been, but I'm reminded of when God created the earth and everything else. He said, 'And it was good.' I pray we'll remember always to ask Him, 'Show us how to live,' so He'll say about this family, 'And it was good.' "

"Amen," Grandfather Gabriel pronounced with several of the other guests, and Ginger had to blink her eyes hard again.

116

"And now," Grant said, "I think it's our guests' duty to finish off this cake!"

"I love cake!" Lilabet piped, and everyone laughed again.

When will they open the new wedding gifts? Ginger wondered. *And when they don't get one from me, will they remember that I didn't want them to get married?*

Mom and Grant left to change into their traveling clothes. They were flying to Seattle for their honeymoon, and Ginger would stay with Gram. Grandfather Gabriel would take care of Joshua and Lilabet.

Finally Mom and Grant returned, Mom in her pale blue going-away suit. She happily announced, "Time to throw the bouquet!" and turned her back to the group of single ladies. "Here goes!" She tossed the bouquet over her shoulder. To her delight, Aunt Rosie caught it.

"Rosie will be the next bride!" Nana Allan sang out.

Will they open the new presents now? Ginger wondered with dismay. Somehow she'd have to explain. Awful as she felt, she made herself step through the crowd to Mom and Grant. Her voice felt all quivery, but she said it anyhow. "I'm sorry. I—I didn't buy you a wedding present."

Her mother's blue eyes widened, then she smiled and kissed Ginger's forehead. "Why . . . we didn't expect one from you."

That very moment, Ginger knew it was the time to tell. She spoke quietly, for the words were so important. "I received Jesus in my heart last week, Mom. I'm a Christian now, too."

Tears burst to her mother's eyes. "Oh, Ginger, that's the best wedding present you could ever give us!"

Grant's nice grayish-blue eyes sparkled with happiness. "How we've been praying for just that!"

They caught her in a great, heartwarming hug. Instead of time zigzagging by as it had all day, it seemed to slow to one wonderful golden moment. And Ginger knew, as they held each other, that they were reflecting God's love.

OFF TO A NEW START

Aoooouuuuh!
Aooooouuuuuh!

The blast of Ginger's conch shell sounds through
the Gabriels' house. But is it a call to battle or a plea
for peace?

Some days Ginger isn't sure, as she struggles to
find her place in her new "combined" family, in her
new school, and as a new child of God. With the
wise counsel of Grandfather Gabriel and the support of her family, Ginger learns some important
lessons about making friends and making peace.

The Ginger Series
    Here Comes Ginger!   A Job for an Angel
    Off to a New Start   Absolutely Green

ELAINE L. SCHULTE is a southern Californian, like Ginger. She has written many stories,
articles, and books for all ages, but the **Ginger
Trumbell Books** is her first series for kids.

Chariot Books™
David C. Cook Publishing Co.

A JOB FOR AN ANGEL

Love your neighbor?

October brings two new people into Ginger's life—and they couldn't be more different from each other.

Ginger looks forward to her Wednesday afternoon job of "baby-sitting" Aunt Alice. She may be elderly and ill, but she's cheerful and fun to be with. At school, however, Ginger is stuck trying to befriend grouchy Robin Lindberg, who never misses an opportunity to be nasty.

Ginger knows that "love your neighbor" includes the Robins as well as the Aunt Alices . . . but knowing doesn't make it easy. . . .

The Ginger Series
   Here Comes Ginger!   A Job for an Angel
   Off to a New Start   Absolutely Green

ELAINE L. SCHULTE is a southern Californian, like Ginger. She has written many stories, articles, and books for all ages, but the **Ginger Trumbell Books** is her first series for kids.

Chariot Books™
David C. Cook Publishing Co.

ABSOLUTELY GREEN

Green with envy— that's Ginger!

Life with her new "combined family" has just begun to feel natural when Ginger's mom and stepdad make an announcement: a new baby is on the way!

They sure are happy about it, but Ginger doesn't know what to think. It's clear that her stepbrother, Joshua, is anything but pleased—and for some reason, the news seems to make him grouchier than ever with Ginger.

Together Ginger's family discovers how God's love can conquer even feelings of resentment and jealousy.

The Ginger Series
Here Comes Ginger!   A Job for an Angel
Off to a New Start   Absolutely Green

ELAINE L. SCHULTE is a southern Californian, like Ginger. She has written many stories, articles, and books for all ages, but the **Ginger Trumbell Books** is her first series for kids.

Chariot Books ™
David C. Cook Publishing Co.

JUST VICTORIA

I am absolutely *dreading* junior high.

Vic and her best friend, Chelsie, have heard enough gory details about seventh grade to ruin their entire summer vacation. And as if school weren't a big enough worry, Vic suddenly finds problems at every turn:

• Chelsie starts hanging around Peggy Hiltshire, queen of all the right cliques, who thinks life revolves around the cheerleading squad.

• Vic's mom gets a "fulfilling" new job—with significantly less pay—at a nursing home.

• Grandma Warden is looking tired and pale—and won't see a doctor.

But Victoria Hope Mahoney has a habit of underestimating her own potential. The summer brings a lot of change, but Vic is equal to it as she learns more about her faith, friendship, and growing up.

Don't miss any books in
The Victoria Mahoney Series!

SHELLY NIELSEN lives in Minneapolis, Minnesota, with her husband and two Yorkshire terriers.

TAKE A BOW, VICTORIA

I might as well die of embarrassment right here.

Victoria is finding plenty to cringe about these days, such as her hugely pregnant mom waddling into the school auditorium in full view of all Vic's friends. (Couldn't she sit quietly at home till the baby arrives?) Or such as Isadora, her flashy grandmother, actually volunteering as set designer for the spring production at school. (Couldn't she bake cookies and knit like a normal grandma?)

Meanwhile Vic is struggling with her own confusing wish to be a star . . . and to stay safely hidden backstage. As some important events change life for the Mahoney family, Vic finds her ideas of stardom—and of courage—changing, too.

Don't miss any books in
The Victoria Mahoney Series!

Just Victoria   Only Kidding, Victoria
More Victoria   Maybe It's Love, Victoria
Take a Bow, Victoria   Autograph, Please,
                                 Victoria

SHELLY NIELSEN lives in Minneapolis, Minnesota, with her husband and two Yorkshire terriers.

AUTOGRAPH PLEASE, VICTORIA

Vickie Mahoney, celebrity?

The weeks before Christmas are exciting ones for Victoria. Winning a national contest brings attention from teachers, an interview on local TV, and a new excuse for best friend, Chelsie, to dream and scheme on Vic's behalf ("Do you want to hear my Vic Mahoney Promotion Plan?").

But Vic is distracted from her stardom by her little brother's big troubles. Matthew's "adjustment problems" in first grade turn out to be a learning disability. Once again the Mahoney family is put to the test, and once again their faith in God, affection for each other, and slightly crazy sense of humor help them survive.

In the process, Vic realizes a little more about who she is and what really matters.

Don't miss any books in The Victoria Mahoney Series!

Just Victoria

More Victoria

Take a Bow, Victoria

Only Kidding, Victoria

Maybe It's Love, Victoria

Autograph, Please, Victoria

SHELLY NIELSEN lives in Minneapolis, Minnesota, with her husband and two Yorkshire terriers.